THE
NARROW ROAD
BETWEEN DESIRES

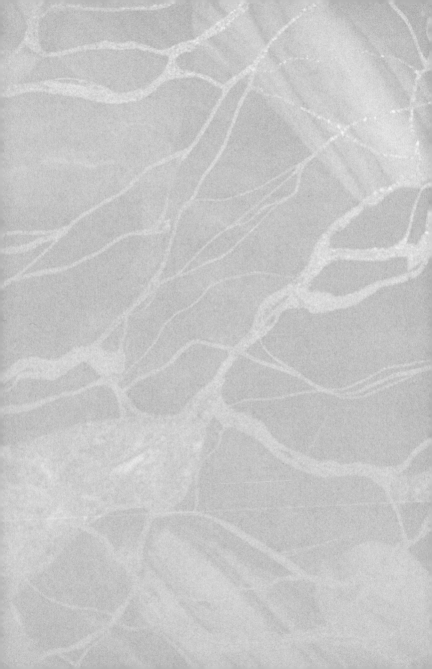

THE
NARROW ROAD
BETWEEN DESIRES

PATRICK ROTHFUSS

ILLUSTRATIONS BY NATE TAYLOR

DAW BOOKS
New York

Jacket image compositing by Adam Auerbach
Moon: Gary Yeowell via Getty Images
Tree: Salva Mira Photography via Getty Images
Clouds: Daniel Garrido via Getty Images
Grass: Milamai via Getty Images

Book design by Alissa Theodor
Edited by Betsy Wollheim
DAW Book Collectors No. 1950

DAW Books
An imprint of Astra Publishing House
dawbooks.com
DAW Books and its logo are registered trademarks of
Astra Publishing House

Printed in the United States of America

Library of Congress Cataloging-in-Publication Data

Names: Rothfuss, Patrick, 1973- author. | Rothfuss, Patrick,
1973- Lightning tree. | Taylor, Nate, illustrator.
Title: The narrow road between desires / Patrick Rothfuss ;
illustrations by Nate Taylor.
Description: First edition. | New York : DAW Books, 2023. |
Series: The kingkiller chronicle
Identifiers: LCCN 2023033076 (print) | LCCN 2023033077 (ebook) |
ISBN 9780756419172 (hardcover) | ISBN 9780756419189 (ebook)
Subjects: LCGFT: Fantasy fiction. | Novels.
Classification: LCC PS3618.O8685 N37 2023 (print) |
LCC PS3618.O8685 (ebook) | DDC 813/.6--dc23/eng/20230718
LC record available at https://lccn.loc.gov/2023033076
LC ebook record available at https://lccn.loc.gov/2023033077

First edition: November 2023
10 9 8 7 6 5 4 3 2 1

For my sweet boys: Oot and Cutie.

*My favorite stories are the ones we tell each other.
You're the best part of my life. You deserve a perfect
father, but I'm glad you have me instead.*

—Pat

*For Grace, who shows me how to be bold and
reminds me of the magic in ordinary things.*

—Nate

AUTHOR'S FOREWORD

You might not want to buy this book.

I know, that's not the sort of thing an author is supposed to say. But I'd rather be honest with you right out of the gate.

First, if you haven't read my other books, you probably don't want to start here.

My first two books are *The Name of the Wind* and *The Wise Man's Fear*. If you're curious to try my writing, start there. They're the best introduction to my words and my world. This book deals with Bast, a character from that series. And while I've done my best to make this story stand on its own, if you start here, you're going to be missing a lot of context.

Second, if you *have* read my other work, you should know a version of this story was published in the beforetimes. Back in the long, long ago. Back before COVID.

Back when Twitter was fun, and the world was green and new.

Which is to say a little less than ten years ago. I published a version of this story under the title "The Lightning Tree" in an anthology called *Rogues*. I talk about this a little in my author's note at the end of the book, but suffice to say that the version you're holding is wildly different: I've obsessively re-written it, added 15,000+ words, and worked with the fabulous Nate Taylor to add over 40 illustrations.

That said, if you read "The Lightning Tree" back in the day, you know the shape of this story. There's much that is different, much changed, much added, but the bones are the same. So if you're looking for something *utterly* new, you're not going to find it here.

On the other hand, if you'd like to learn more about Bast, this book has a lot to offer. If you're curious about faerie bargains and the secret desires hearts can hold. If you're curious about magics only glimpsed in my other books. If you want to know more about what Bast does in his spare time in the small town of Newarre . . . .

Well, then this book might be for you.

DAWN: ARTISTRY

BAST ALMOST MADE it out the back door of the Waystone Inn.

Technically, he *had* made it outside. Both feet were over the threshold and the door was only a crack away from being closed.

Then he heard his master's voice and went perfectly still. He knew he hadn't given himself away. He was intimate with every subtle sound the inn could make. Not just the simple tricks a child would think clever: carrying their shoes, leaving creaky doors open ahead of time, muffling footsteps on a rug . . . .

No. Bast was better than that. He could move through a room barely stirring the air. He knew which stairs sighed when it had rained the night before, which windows opened easy and which shutters caught the wind. He could tell when a detour out and over the peak of the roof would make less noise than the straight way through the upper hall.

That would be enough for some. But on the rare occasion when he actually cared, Bast found success as dull as ditchwater. Let others settle for mere excellence. Bast was an artist.

Because of this, Bast knew true silence was unnatural. To a careful ear, silence sounded like a knife in the dark.

So when Bast glided through the empty inn, he played the floorboards like an instrument. A sigh, a pause, a click, a creak. Sounds that would catch a guest just drifting off to sleep. But to someone who lived there . . . it was nothing. It was *less* than nothing. It was the comfortable sound of heavy timber bones settling slowly into earth, easy to ignore as a familiar lover stirring next to you in bed.

Knowing all this, Bast eyed the door. He kept the bright brass hinges oiled, but even so he shifted his grip and lifted so the door's weight didn't hang. Only then did he ease it slowly closed. A moth would make more noise.

Bast stood to his full height and grinned, his face sweet and sly and wild. In that moment, he looked less like a rakish young man, and more a naughty child who had stolen the moon and planned to eat it like a thin, pale silver cake. His smile was like the final crescent of remaining moon, sharp and white and dangerous.

"Bast!" The call came from the inn again, louder this time. Nothing so crass as a shout. His master did not bellow like a farmer calling cows, but his voice could carry like a hunting horn. Bast felt it tug him like a hand around his heart.

Bast sighed, then opened the door and strode briskly back inside. He made walking look like dancing. He was dark, and tall, and lovely. When he scowled, his face was still more sweet than others might look smiling. "Yes Reshi?" he called brightly.

After a moment the innkeeper stepped into the kitchen. He wore a clean white apron and his hair was red. His face held the stolid placidness of bored innkeepers everywhere. Despite the early hour, he looked tired.

He handed Bast a leather-bound book. "You almost forgot this," he said without a hint of sarcasm.

Bast made a show of looking surprised. "Oh! Thank you, Reshi!"

"No bother, Bast." The innkeeper's mouth made the shape of a smile. "While you're out today, would you mind picking up some eggs?"

Bast nodded, tucking the book under his arm. "Anything else?" he asked.

"Maybe some carrots too? I'm thinking we'll do stew tonight. It's Felling, so we'll need to be ready for a crowd." His mouth turned up slightly at one corner as he said this.

"Eggs and carrots," Bast repeated dutifully.

The innkeeper started to turn away, then stopped. "Oh, the Tilman boy stopped by yesterday, looking for you."

Bast tilted his head to one side, his expression puzzled.

"I think he's Jessom's son?" the innkeeper provided, holding up a hand to roughly chest height. "Dark hair? Name was . . ." He trailed off, narrowing his eyes as he tried to remember.

"Rike." Bast dropped the name like a lump of hot iron, then pressed on quickly, hoping his master wouldn't notice. "Tilmans are the woodcutters off to the south of town. No wives or kids. Was it Rike Williams? Dark eyes. Grubby?" Bast thought a moment, wondering how else he might describe the boy. "Probably looked nervous? Like he was making a point of not stealing anything?"

The last brought a glimmer of recognition to the innkeeper's face, and he nodded. "Said he was looking for you, but didn't leave any sort of message . . ." He raised an eyebrow at Bast. The look said more than it said.

"I haven't the slightest idea what he wants," Bast said, sounding honest. He was being honest, too. But better than anyone, Bast knew what *that* was worth. All that glittered wasn't gilt, and sometimes it was worth a little work so that you seemed to be the thing you truly were.

Nodding, the innkeeper made a noncommittal noise and moved back toward the common room. If he said anything further, Bast didn't hear it, as he was already running lightly through the dewy grass and the startling blue-grey light of dawn.

MORNING: EMBRIL

BY THE TIME Bast arrived, the sun was peering up above the trees, painting the few thin clouds with pale shades of pink and violet.

Two children were already waiting in the clearing. They kept a respectful distance from the top of the hill, playing on the huge greystone that lay half-fallen at the bottom, climbing up the side, then jumping down to land laughing in the tall grass.

Knowing they were watching, Bast took his time climbing the tiny hill. At the top stood what the children called the lightning tree, though these days all that remained was a broad, broken, branchless trunk. The original tree must have been vast, as even this remnant was so tall that Bast could barely reach the top.

The bark had long since fallen away, and years of sun had bleached the bare wood white as bone except for all along its ragged top. There, even after all these years, the wood was a deep and jagged black. Trailing down the remaining trunk, the lightning had charred a wild, dark, forking image of itself into the bone-white wood, as if to sign its work.

Bast reached out with his left hand, touching the smooth trunk with his fingertips as he slowly walked a circle around the tree. He walked widdershins, turning against the world. The way of breaking. Three times.

Then he switched hands and paced around the tree in the opposite direction, moving the same way as the turning sun. Three slow circles deasil. The proper way for making. Thus he went while the children watched, back and forth, as if the tree were a bobbin he was winding and unwinding.

Finally Bast sat and rested his back against the tree. He lay the book on a nearby stone, the rising sun shone red against the hammered gold of the title: *Celum Tinture.*

Then Bast amused himself by tossing stones down into the stream that cut sharply into the slope of the hill opposite the greystone.

After a minute, a round-faced blonde girl trudged up the hill. She was the baker's youngest daughter, Brann. She smelled of sweat and bread and . . . something else. Something out of place.

The girl's slow approach had an air of ritual about it. She crested the small hill and stood there for a moment, the only noise coming from the other children gathered below, gone back to playing.

Finally Bast turned his head and looked the girl over. No more than nine, she was a little more well-dressed and well-fed than most of the town's other children. She carried a wad of white cloth in her hand.

The girl stepped forward, swallowing nervously. "I need a lie."

Bast nodded, his face impassive. "What sort?"

Brann gingerly opened her hand, revealing a shock of red staining the cloth. It stuck to her hand slightly, a makeshift bandage. Bast nodded, realizing what he'd smelled before.

"I was playing with my mum's knives," Brann said, embarrassed.

Bast held out his hand and the girl took a few steps closer. Bast unwrapped the cloth with his long fingers and examined the cut. It ran along the meat near the thumb. Not too deep. "Hurt much?"

"Nothing like the birching I'll get if she finds out I was messing with her knives," Brann muttered.

Bast looked up at her. "You clean the knife and put it back?"

Brann nodded.

Bast tapped his lips thoughtfully. "You thought you saw a big black rat. It scared you. You threw a knife at it and cut yourself. Yesterday one of the other children told you a story about rats chewing off soldier's ears and toes while they slept. It gave you nightmares."

Brann gave a shudder. "Who told me the story?"

Bast shrugged off the question. "Pick someone you don't like."

The girl grinned viciously.

Bast began to tick off things on his fingers. "Get some fresh blood on the knife before you throw it." He pointed at the cloth the girl had wrapped her hand in. "Get rid of that, too. The blood is dry, and obviously old. Can you work up a good cry?"

The girl seemed a little abashed and shook her head.

11

"Put some salt in your eyes," Bast said matter-of-factly. "Maybe a little pepper up your nose? Get all snotty and teary before you run to them. Then," Bast held up a cautionary finger. "Try *not* to cry. Don't sniffle. Don't blink. When they ask you about your hand, tell your mum you're sorry if you broke her knife."

Brann listened, nodding slowly at first, then faster. She smiled. "That's good." She looked around nervously. "What do I owe you?"

"Any secrets?" Bast asked.

The baker's girl thought for a minute. "Widow Creel is tupping the miller's husband?" she said hopefully.

Bast waved his hand as if shooing away a fly. "For years. That's not a secret," he said. "Everyone knows, including his wife." He rubbed his nose. "What have you got in your pockets?"

The girl dug around and held up her uninjured hand. It held a tangle of string, two iron shims, a flat green stone, a blue button, and a bird's skull.

Bast took the string. Then, careful not to touch the shims, he plucked the green stone out from among the rest. It was a flat, irregular shape, carved with the face of a sleeping woman. "Is this an embril?" he asked, looking surprised.

Brann shrugged. "Looks like part of a Telgim Set to me. They're for telling fortunes."

Bast held the stone up to the light. "Where'd you get it?"

"I traded it off Rike," Brann said. "Said it was an ordal, but . . . he only . . . ."

Bast's eyes narrowed at the boy's name, his mouth making a flat line.

Belatedly realizing her mistake, Brann went still. The girl's eyes darted around nervously. "I . . ." She licked her lips nervously. "You asked . . . ."

His expression sour, Bast looked down at the stone as if it had started to smell. He briefly considered throwing it down into the stream from pure spite.

Then, thinking better of it, he flipped it up into the air like a coin instead. Catching it, he opened his hand to reveal the other side of the stone. On this side, the carved woman's eyes were open, and she smiled.

Bast rubbed it between his fingers thoughtfully. "This then. And a sweet bun every day for a full span."

"That emerel or whatever," Brann said, "*and* the string you took, and I'll bring you one bun later today, warm out of the oven." Brann's expression was firm, but her voice turned up at the end.

"Two buns," Bast countered. "So long as they're maple, not molasses."

After a moment's hesitation, the girl nodded. "What if I get a birching anyway?" she asked.

"That's your business." Bast shrugged. "You wanted a lie. I gave you a good one. If you want me to haul you out of trouble personally? That's a different deal entirely."

The baker's girl looked a little disappointed, but she turned and headed down the hill.

Next up the hill was one of the Alard boys. There were an uncountable ruck of them, formed by several families constantly blending and merging. The lot of them looked similar enough that Bast struggled to remember which was which.

This one looked as furious as only a boy of ten can be. He wore tattered homespun and had a split lip and a crust of blood around one nostril. "I caught my brother kissing Grett behind the old mill!" the boy said as soon as he crested the hill, not waiting for Bast to ask. "He knew I was sweet on 'em!"

Bast spread his hands and looked around helplessly, shrugging.

"Revenge," the boy spat.

"Public revenge?" Bast asked. "Or secret revenge?"

The boy touched his split lip with his tongue. "Secret revenge," he said in a low voice.

Something about the gesture jogged Bast's memory, this was Kale. He'd once tried to trade Bast a pair of frogs for "a curse that would make someone fart forever." Negotiations had grown heated before falling apart. He was thicker than a prince's porridge, but Bast still held a grudging admiration for the boy.

"How much revenge?" Bast asked.

The boy thought for a bit, then held up his hands about two feet apart. "This much."

"Hmm," Bast said. "How much on a scale from mouse to bull?"

The boy rubbed his nose. "About a cat's worth," he said. "Maybe a dog's worth. Not like Crazy Martin's dogs though. Like the Bentons' dogs."

Bast tilted his head back in a thoughtful way. "Okay," he said. "Piss in his shoes."

The boy looked skeptical. "That don't sound like a whole dog's worth of revenge."

Bast made a calming motion with the hand holding the green stone. "You piss in a cup and hide it. Let it sit for a day or two. Then one night when he's put his shoes by the fire, pour the piss on his shoes. Don't make a puddle, just get them a little damp. In the morning they'll be dry and probably won't even smell—"

"Then what's the point?" Kale burst out, throwing his hands into the air. "That's not a flea's worth of revenge!"

Continuing as if the boy hadn't spoken, Bast said. "Do it for three nights. Don't get caught. Don't overdo it. Just get them a little damp so they're dry by morning."

Bast held up a hand before Kale could interrupt. "After that, whenever his feet get sweaty, he'll start to smell a little like piss." Bast watched Kale's face as he continued. "He steps in a puddle? He smells like piss. Morning dew gets his feet wet? He'll smell a little like piss."

"Just a little?" Kale said, baffled.

Bast gave a gusty, exaggerated sigh. "That way, it will be easy for him to miss and hard for him to figure out where it's coming from. And because it's just a little, he'll get used to it."

The boy looked thoughtful.

"And you know how old piss smells worse and worse? He'll stay used to it, but other folk won't." Bast grinned at the boy. "I'm guessing Grett isn't going to want to kiss the kid who can't stop pissing himself."

Admiration spread across the young boy's face like

sunrise. "That's the most bastardy thing I've ever heard," he said.

Bast tried to look modest and failed. "Have you got anything for me?"

"I found a wild bee hive," the boy said.

"That will do for a start," Bast said. "Where?"

"It's off past the Orrisons.' Past Littlecreek." The boy squatted down and with just a few quick strokes drew a surprisingly clear map in the dirt. "See?"

Bast nodded. "Anything else?"

"Well . . . ." He looked up and to the side. "I know where Crazy Martin keeps his still."

Bast raised his eyebrows. "Really?"

The boy stepped to the side then knelt down and connected another map to the first, drawing almost absentmindedly while he spoke. "You cross this bit of the river twice," he said. "Then you'll want to go around the outcrop, because it looks like you can't climb it. But there's a little trail you can't see." He added one more line in the dirt, then squinted up at Bast. "We square?"

Bast studied the map, then ran a hand over it briskly, obscuring the lines. "We're square."

"Got a message for you too." The boy stood and dusted off his knees. "Rike says he wants to meet."

Bast's mouth made a thin and bloodless line. "Rike knows the rules." Bast's voice was grim, just saying the name felt like a fishbone stuck halfway down his throat. "Tell him no."

"I already told him," Kale said, lifting his shoulders all the way up to his ears in an exaggerated shrug. "But I'll tell him again if I see him. . . ."

••••◉••••

After that, Bast tucked *Celum Tinture* under his arm and went on a rambling stroll. He found wild raspberries and ate them. He hopped a fence to drink from the Ostlars' well and pet their dog. He found an interesting stick, and used it to poke at things until he knocked down a hornet's nest that wasn't quite as abandoned as he thought. In his scramble to get away, he lost the stick, slipped on a slope of loose rock, and tore a hole in the knee of his pants.

Eventually Bast climbed to the top of a bluff where an ancient twisted holly tree stretched against the sky. He tucked the leather-bound book snugly against a branch, before reaching into a round hollow in the trunk. After a moment, he pulled out a small dark bundle that fit in the palm of his hand.

Unfolding the bundle revealed it to be a sack of soft, dark leather. He worked the drawstring loose and dropped the smooth green embril inside. It made a muffled *tic* like a marble against marbles.

He was about to return the sack then considered for a moment before sitting cross-legged on the ground. He brushed leaves and twigs aside, then put his hand inside the sack and stirred the contents idly. It made an odd, complex sound of wood and stone and metal jostling against each other.

Bast closed his eyes, held his breath, then drew out a hand and tossed the contents into the air.

Opening his eyes, Bast watched four embrils tumble down. Three of them made a rough triangle: A piece of pale horn carved with a crescent moon, a clay disk with a stylized wave, and a piece of tile painted with a dancing piper. Outside the triangle was something that looked like half an iron coin, but wasn't.

Bast looked down at them, frowning slightly. Then he closed his eyes again and held his breath before making another pull, tossing it into the air as well. It fell between the horn and clay embrils, a flat piece of white wood with a spindle carved so the grain of the wood gave the impression of wound thread.

Bast's brow furrowed. He looked up at the sky, clear and bright. Not much wind. Warm but not hot. Hadn't rained for a span of days. Hours before noon on Felling. Wasn't a market day . . . .

Nodding, he swept the pieces back into their sack. Down past Old Lant's place, around the brambles that bordered the Alard farm until he came to a marshy bit of Littlecreek where he cut a handful of reeds with a small, bright knife. He found a piece of string in his pocket, and quickly bound them together into a tidy set of shepherd's pipes.

He blew across the reeds and cocked his head at their sweet discord. His bright knife flashed, and he tested the reeds again. This time they sounded almost true, which made the discord far more grating. There was a lesson there.

The blade flicked again. Once. Twice. Thrice. Not bothering to test the sound again, Bast tucked the knife away. He eyed the side of his finger where the knife had grazed him, leaving a line so thin you'd think the cut came from a blade of grass. Then the blood welled up, red as a poppy.

Bast put his finger in his mouth, then brought the pipes up to his face and breathed in deep through his nose, smelling the wet green of the reeds. He wet his lips and licked the fresh-cut tops of the reeds, the flicker of his tongue a sudden, startling red.

Then he drew a breath and blew against the pipes. This time the sound was bright as moonlight. Lively as a leaping fish. Sweet as stolen fruit. Lowering the pipes, he heard the low, mindless bleat of distant sheep.

Cresting the hill, Bast saw two dozen fat, daft sheep cropping grass in the valley below. It was shadowy here, secluded. The steep sides of the valley meant the sheep weren't in danger of straying. Even the sheepdog was spread out lazily on a warm rock, dozing.

A young man sat beneath a spreading elm that overlooked the valley, his long shepherd's crook leaned against the tree. He had taken off his shoes, and his hat was low over his eyes. He wore green trousers, loose at the leg, and a bright yellow shirt that suited the richly tanned skin of his face and arms. His long, thick hair was the color of ripe wheat.

Bast began playing as he made his way down the hill. A dangerous tune, low and slow and sly as a gentle breeze.

The shepherd perked up at the sound of it. He lifted his head, excited . . . but no. Apparently it was something else he heard, as he didn't look in Bast's direction at all.

He did climb to his feet though. It wasn't particularly hot, but he fanned himself with his hat, then slowly removed his yellow shirt, using it to mop his brow before hanging it on a nearby branch. Then he stretched, hands twining over his head as the muscles of his shoulders and back played against each other.

Bast's tune changed a bit, growing bright and light as water running over stones.

The nearby sheepdog lifted his head at the sound, stared at Bast for a moment, then lay it back down on the stone, utterly uninterested.

The shepherd on the other hand, gave no indication he could hear it. Though the young man picked up a nearby blanket and spread it beneath the tree. Which was a little odd, as he had been sitting in the same place before without it. Perhaps he'd grown chilly, now that he'd taken off his shirt. . . . Yes. Surely that was it.

Bast continued to play as he walked down the slope.

The music he made was sweet and playful and languid all at once.

Sitting down on the blanket, the shepherd leaned back and shook his head slightly. His long, honey-colored hair fell away from his shoulders, exposing the lovely line of his neck, from his perfect shell-like ear down to the broad expanse of his chest.

Watching intently as he made his way down the hill, Bast stepped on a loose stone and stumbled awkwardly. He blew a hard, squawking note, then dropped a few more from his song as he threw out an arm wildly to catch his balance.

The shepherd laughed then. At first it seemed as if he must be laughing at Bast . . . but no. Obviously that wasn't the case, as he was pointedly looking in the other direction. He was covering his mouth, too. It had probably been a cough. Or perhaps the sheep had done something humorous. Yes. That was surely it. They could be funny animals at times.

But one can only look at sheep for so long. The shepherd sighed and relaxed, reclining on the blanket. Putting one arm behind his head made the muscles of his arms and shoulders flex. He stretched lazily, arching his back a bit. The sunlight dappling through the leaves showed the roundness of his chest and belly was covered in the lightest down of honey-colored hair.

Bast continued down the hill toward where the shepherd lay, his steps delicate and graceful. He looked like a stalking cat. He looked like he was dancing.

The shepherd sighed again and closed his eyes, his face tilted like a flower to catch the sun. For all that he looked like he was trying to sleep, his breath seemed to be coming rather quickly. Shifting restlessly, he ran a hand through his hair, splaying it out on the blanket. He bit his lower lip . . . .

It is difficult to grin while playing shepherd's pipes. But Bast was something of an artist.

MID-MORNING:
THE NARROW ROAD

THE SUN HAD climbed a bit by the time Bast returned to
the lightning tree. He was pleasantly sweaty with his hair
in a state of mild dishevel, but the torn knee of his pants
had been carefully mended with small, even stitches. The
thread was an off-color white against the dark fabric, but
the seam had been cleverly worked into the shape of a
shepherd's crook, and a small fluffy sheep had been embroidered further up the leg.

There were no children waiting, so Bast did a quick
circle of the tree, once in each direction to ensure his

workings were still firm. Then he brought out the folded-over leather sack, sat down against the tree, and made a pull. Opening his hand, he frowned to see the embril that looked very like a broken coin. Irritated, he put it back and drew again. This time he seemed more pleased to find a wooden square painted with a tiny sleeping fox.

Bast tried to walk the wooden embril down his knuckles like a coin and failed. Then he flipped it in the air with his thumb, caught it, and slapped it on his wrist, revealing the sleeping fox again. Smiling, he leaned his head against the smooth white side of the lightning tree, and was snoring softly in half a moment's time.

••••❀•••••

Bast blinked himself awake at the sound of footsteps clomping up the hill. Blearily, he peered at the position of the sun and stretched. Then, looking down the hill, he smiled to see a blue-eyed boy with freckles.

"Kostrel!" Bast called happily. "How is the road to Tinuë?"

"Sunny!" the boy said, smiling back as he came to the top of the hill, revealing well-worn boots a bit too big for him. He cut a sly look sideways at Bast and lowered his voice conspiratorially. "I have something for you!"

Bast made a show of rubbing his hands together with delight.

"In fact," Kostrel continued with a touch of drama, "I have *three* things for you today." He looked around casually, his eye sweeping the bottom of the hill where no children were waiting. "If you have time, that is. I know you tend to be busy . . . ."

Bast stretched lazily to draw the moment out. Kostrel bargained like a friendly ivy, cheerfully finding the slenderest crack where he could gain purchase. Bast wasn't fool enough to give him even a slight advantage by asking what he'd brought.

But he also wanted time to give Kostrel a second look, sensing something slightly off. Were his shoulders tight? His smile a little wide? Was the boy nervous, or just a bit more excited than usual?

"That's the trouble with giving people what they need," Bast said slowly, matching Kostrel's indifferent tone. "They don't need to come back for more."

Bast fought the urge to smile as he let the conversation lull. He saw Kostrel fidget with a loose thread on his shirt cuff, then rock onto the balls of his feet. The boy was sharp, but still so young. Not anxious then. Eager. He must have something good to trade.

It was barely two breaths before Kostrel cracked and spoke. "First we have a gift," he said, and with great ceremony, he dipped a hand into his pocket and brought out a closed fist concealing something.

"I don't go in for presents as a rule," Bast said dubiously. Despite his tone, his eyes were fixed on Kostrel's outstretched hand.

Grinning, Kostrel moved his closed hand back and forth in a teasing way. He waggled his eyebrows ridiculously.

Bast smiled as he felt the old familiar tug inside. He

wasn't wise, but he had been burned before, and wary was wisdom's cousin. Still, his curiosity itched at him. . . .

But no. Bast had not the least desire to be bound. Even a thimbleful of obligation rankled him. Even to a sunny summer child like this.

That said . . . it was almost surely nothing dangerous. Just some bauble. A button. An odd tooth he stumbled on while digging. A spinning top. An interesting rock shaped slightly like a dog. No *real* harm came from taking gifts like those. The debt they hung was lighter than a pin.

But then again, what if the button were of bone? What if there were a ruby hidden unseen in the stone? What if the toy had been adored? Cherished, cared for, generations old? Passed from hand to hand with love, heavy as a shackle made of gold?

No. Certainly not. It simply wasn't worth the risk.

So Bast resisted. Shaking his head, he leaned back and crossed his arms. Even so, his eyes flicked back to the boy's hand, there and away, quick as a snake's tongue darting out to taste the air.

Kostrel started to rock back and forth in an improvised dance, humming and wiggling both eyebrows all at

once. He waggled his hips and waved the arm he wasn't leaving tantalizingly outstretched to Bast.

There was a reason Kostrel was his favorite. He was a perfect mix of cleverness and fool. He looked so ridiculous Bast relented, laughing. "I suppose I can make a rare exception. Just for you."

Then, against his wit and will, but following his heart, Bast reached out and held his open hand beneath the boy's clenched fist.

Kostrel stopped his clowning long enough to open up his hand. A bit of metal tumbled down. A tiny teardrop flashed and glittered, caught the sun, and spun . . .

It landed on Bast's palm as lightly as a leaf. It struck him like an anvil on his heart. It drove the breath from him like he'd been pushed deep underwater. It left him stunned as if the tree behind him had been hit with lightning twice despite the clear blue sky above.

Bast's vision dimmed. The world went grey then faded further almost into black until the only piece of light remaining came from the tiny sun-touched tearlike bit of brass held in his hand. Before he could see more, his fingers clenched around it as if taken by a sudden cramp.

The world snapped back. Light and color. Wind. The smell of grass.

Reeling, Bast made certain his face was still a mask. It held. He made certain it showed nothing of his eyes or what he truly felt. Then he flourished it with just a tinge of curiosity, lifting up one eyebrow just a bit.

Kostrel watched him eagerly, and Bast's first thought was that the quickest way to fix the clever little bastard's trick would be to rip his throat clean out and throw him off the hill. He'd strike the hard stone bluff across the water, then fall into the stream below. Bast would like to see the spiteful little viper try to call his name without a voice, a shattered back, and lungs fast filling up with water running swift against . . . .

But of course he couldn't. That was the first of many things Bast would be barred from doing now that he'd been fool enough to take a gift not knowing what it was, not knowing how much obligation it would hang around his neck, or how heavy it would press down on his heart. A gift unseen, as if he were some dewy, day-old dennerling.

"I thought you might not have set your eyes on one of those before," Kostrel said. His tone was one part smug, two parts delight.

Bast began to seethe. But the boy's expression . . . something in it wasn't right. The trap was sprung, but Kostrel didn't show a hint of gloat. No wicked glee. No sharp relief. No excitement at the certain knowledge his trick had worked. Kostrel simply didn't have the proper look. A budding Tarsus ought to stroke his chin and laugh a bit, or at least have the decency to look superior and self-satisfied.

Moving carefully to keep his mask in place, Bast tried to reach his hand out to the boy. Much to his surprise, he found he could. Slowly Bast put two fingers lightly onto Kostrel's arm. No resistance thickened the air. He felt no pain, no dread. His vision didn't dim. Nothing. For some reason he could still lay hands upon the boy.

Bast leaned forward slightly, and quickly as a striking snake, he put one hand around the young boy's throat. Still nothing. Bast felt the boy's pulse tap tenderly against his fingertips.

With a bubbling giggle, Kostrel pulled away. It was a bashful motion, without a hint of startlement or fear. "Do they say 'thanks' by tickling folk where you come from?" he mumbled, rubbing the side of his neck shyly, looking around as if embarrassed someone might have seen. "Stop it, Bast."

At the sound of his name, Bast tensed. But there was nothing. No compulsion. No weakness. No feeling like Kostrel held a leash pulled tight around his throat . . .

Baffled, Bast looked down at his clenched fist. This was no mere button or beloved toy. Despite what stories said, it was no simple thing to truly bind one such as Bast. And the list of things that could do so as sudden, hard, and heavy as this gift had managed was short indeed. Grandfather iron would work, of course. Or a piece of star that fell to earth. One of a handful of dark and ancient links of broken chain. . . .

But those were dark, and what he'd glimpsed was bright.

A seal of sovereign gold might work, but only with the proper names. A ring of amber was an older trick, but Bast hadn't seen one in a mortal age. Besides, he would have had to put it on his finger. . . .

Slowly, Bast worked to open up his clenched hand and saw a tiny piece of bright, engraven brass shaped like a tear. Some amulet? A coin?

Bast was puzzled. He didn't recognize the thing, but the sensation wasn't something you forgot. Gingerly, he felt inside himself . . . and there it was. Undeniable as an iron shackle welded tight around his heart. Bast found himself straining to fill his lungs as if he couldn't breathe. But he could. His lungs were full.

With a great effort, Bast forced himself to exhale. Then he drew another lungful, feeling breathless though the air came easy. He'd almost rather it had been some piece of terrible and ancient iron, then at least he'd understand. Bad enough that Kostrel's gift had bound him up with an obligation heavier than he had felt in ages, but what did it mean that the boy couldn't compel him? How could he hope to balance out a debt he didn't even seem to owe to. . . .

Bast looked up at Kostrel's freckled, grinning face. It dawned on him then, and he remembered the exact words the boy had used before. "I see," Bast said slowly. "It's a gift, but not from you. Who is it from then?" Bast asked the question, but he already knew. Full of dread and breathless, he hoped that it wasn't true.

"It was Rike," Kostrel admitted, looking a little sheepish. "That's the second thing I brought. He sent a message. He wants to talk." Kostrel bobbed his shoulders up and down as if shrugging multiple times. "Don't worry, I know the rules and already told him that your answer would be no."

Bast fought the urge to howl and pound his fists into the ground. He fought the urge to sigh and slump with visible relief. Better beholden to a stupid enemy than to a clever friend. Rike had the hungry cunning of a feral dog, but he couldn't have accomplished this on purpose. Far better caught by stupid luck, than have Kostrel somehow spot Bast for what he was, puzzle out the way to bind him, then play the game so sly that he could catch Bast unawares. . . .

So it was bad, but not so bad as he had feared. Bast looked over at the freckled boy, glad he hadn't misjudged Kostrel either.

Bast held the warm brass between his fingers. It showed a pair of hands around a head of wheat. "So what's this then?" he asked. "When it's not out beneath the moon?"

"It's called a penance piece," Kostrel burst out, making it obvious he'd been desperately waiting to be asked. "I went and asked Abbe Leodin cause of the church writing on the bottom." He pointed excitedly. "See?"

Bast turned the coin over. The other side showed a tower wrapped in flame. "Ah," he said grimly. "Of course. *Tehus antausa eha*." He said the words with the light-hearted joy of a man chewing a mouthful of salt.

"I don't know about where you come from," Kostrel continued, "but we shout that at demons come midwinter. It's holy or somesuch. Abbe showed me a few others from the pauper box." He peered down at the coin and shrugged. "Those were different though. He said that one was proper old. But I don't know. It's bright as a new penny. The others were all dull."

Bast continued turning the coin in his fingers, nodding to himself as if listening to someone explain a not particularly funny joke. His mood didn't seem to be notably improved by mention of the priest.

Kostrel chattered on, happily filling the silence. "He said rich folk give them out to beggars to get right with god. But mostly in big cities like Baedn and Atur and such."

Kostrel waved vaguely in the direction of the king's road. "He says any baker in the corners will trade one for a loaf no matter wh . . . ." Kostrel trailed off, seeing Bast's expression.

"Bread!" Bast bit the word off. His tone seething. "That little liar thinks he can buy me off with bread?"

Kostrel's smile fell away, looking startled. "A gift!" he said quickly. "Not a bribe! Rike said it was a gift!"

Bast felt the muscles in his jaw jump as he clenched his teeth. Bast would have been delighted by a bribe. But it wasn't the boy's fault he didn't know. In fact, Kostrel not understanding was the only good part of this entire situation.

Kostrel tried again, his voice high and hesitant. "I don't think he meant anything by it," he said. "Except, y'know. Maybe trying to make things just a little right? He knows he put his foot in it last year, so now he's . . ." He gestured at the coin. "Penance."

After another moment, Kostrel steadied himself and continued. "I mean . . . a loaf might not be much to you, but you live at an inn." Kostrel looked down, uncomfortable. "Most folk don't. For Rike . . . a loaf's not nothing."

Bast turned the bright brass in his fingers again, his

face dark as stormclouds. Still, done was done. He gestured with the coin, then dropped it in the leather sack and cinched it tight. "You think this means I should loosen up his laces?"

Kostrel held his hands out in front of himself. "I do not think one single thing," he said with absolute certainty. "If you two start pissing at each other again, I want to be anywhere other than standing in between!"

Bast burst out laughing and smiled. It was like the sun emerging from behind a cloud. "That is because you are wise beyond your years," he said. "What's the third thing that you brought for me?"

Kostrel relaxed and sat cross-legged on the grass. "I've got a secret to trade," he said. "And I came to you first, because it's valuable information." He hesitated, drawing out the drama of the moment. "I know where Emberlee takes her bath."

Bast raised an interested eyebrow. "Is that so?"

Kostrel rolled his eyes. "You faker. Don't pretend you don't care."

"Of course I care," Bast said with just a hint of wounded pride. "She's the sixth prettiest girl in town, after all."

"Sixth?" the boy said, indignant. "She's the second prettiest and you know it!"

"Perhaps fourth," Bast conceded. "After Annia."

"Annia's legs are skinny as a chicken's," Kostrel said, rolling his eyes.

Bast shrugged lazily. "To each his own. But yes. I am interested. What would you like in trade? An answer, a favor?"

"I want good answers to three questions *and* a favor," the boy said, his dark eyes sharp. "And we both know it's worth it. Because Emberlee is the third prettiest girl in town."

Bast opened his mouth as if he were going to protest, then shrugged instead. "No favor. Three answers on a single subject named beforehand," he countered.

Kostrel chewed his lip. "But if you don't know enough about the subject, I get to pick another."

Bast nodded and held up a finger. "Any subject except that of my employer, of course, whose trust in me I cannot in good conscience betray." Bast's voice was thick with poorly hidden self-importance as he spoke.

Kostrel didn't even bother to dismiss the ridiculous idea that he might be interested in the man who ran the second-most successful taproom in a town so small it only had one inn. "Three full, honest answers," he said. "No equivocating or bullshittery."

"So long as the questions are focused and specific," Bast countered. "No *'tell me everything you know about'* nonsense."

"That wouldn't be a question," Kostrel pointed out.

"Exactly," Bast said. "Three full, honest answers on a single subject. And you agree not to tell anyone else where Emberlee is having her bath." Kostrel scowled at that, and Bast laughed. "You little cocker, you would have sold it twenty times, wouldn't you?"

The boy shrugged easily, not denying it and not embarrassed either. "It's valuable information."

"And you won't show up yourself."

The dark-eyed boy spat a couple words that surprised Bast more than his earlier use of *equivocating.* "Fine," he growled. "But if you don't know the answer to my question, I get to ask another."

Bast thought about it for a moment. "That's fair."

"*And* you loan me another book," the boy said, his dark eyes glaring. "And you give me a copper penny. And you have to describe her breasts to me."

Bast threw back his head and laughed. "Done. If she gives her permission, of course."

Kostrel boggled. "How in twelve different colored hells am I supposed to get her to agree to that?" he asked.

Bast spread his hands helplessly. "Not my problem," he said. "But asking her seems like the straightest road."

Kostrel took a deep breath and let it out again. Then he climbed to his feet, took a step, and pressed a hand against the sun-bleached side of the lightning tree. Bast reached behind his head to touch the tree, and sealed the deal by shaking with the boy. Kostrel's hand was as delicate as a bird's wing inside his own.

Letting go, Bast blinked in the warm sun and started to yawn. "So. What subject are you curious about today?"

Kostrel stepped back and sat on the ground, his serious look shifted into one of giddy excitement. "I want to know about the Fae!"

It's hard to yawn and stretch when it feels like you've swallowed a lump of hot iron. But it was not for nothing Bast considered himself an artist. He seamlessly unspooled his stretch like a cat napping on a warm stone hearth. His yawn was so languid he wished someone was here to see how seamlessly he managed seeming calm.

"Well?" Kostrel asked. "Do you know enough about them?"

"A fair amount," Bast said modestly. "More than most folk, I imagine."

Kostrel's freckled face was triumphant. "I knew it! You aren't from around here. You've seen what's really out there in the world!"

"Some," Bast admitted. He looked up at the sun. "Ask your questions then. I have an important appointment in about an hour."

The boy looked down at the grass for a moment, thinking. "What are they like?"

Bast blinked, then he laughed and threw up his hands. "Merciful Tehlu! Do you have any idea how crazy that question is? They're not *like* anything. They're like themselves."

Kostrel looked indignant. "Don't you try and shim me!" he said, leveling a finger at Bast. "I said no bullshittery!"

"I'm not." Bast raised his hands defensively. "It's just impossible to answer. What would you say if I asked you what *people* were like? How could you answer that? There's so many kinds of people. They're all different."

"So it's a big question," Kostrel said. "Give me a big answer."

"It's not just big," Bast protested. "It would fill a book."

A cat can look at a king, and a kid can climb a tree.

And Kostrel, apparently, could meet Bast's eyes without flinching, blinking, or looking open to the thinnest thread of compromise.

Bast scowled at him. "It could be argued your question is neither focused nor specific."

Kostrel raised an eyebrow. "So we're arguing? I thought we were trading information? If you asked me where Emberlee was going for her bath, and I said, 'in a stream' you'd feel like I'd measured you pretty short corn, wouldn't you?"

Bast sighed. "If I tell you every rumor I've heard, this would take a span of days. And it would be useless, untrue, or contradictory. I promised you answers both honest and true."

Kostrel narrowed his eyes and gave a profoundly unsympathetic shrug. "Not my problem."

Bast held up his hands in surrender. "Here's what I'll do. *Despite* the unfocused nature of your question. I'll give you an answer that covers the rough shape of things and . . ." Bast hesitated. ". . . one true secret relating to the subject. Fair?"

"Two secrets." Kostrel's dark eyes were still serious, but they glittered with excitement, too.

"Okay." Bast looked up at the sky, as if organizing

his thoughts. "When you say 'fae,' you're talking about anything that lives in the Fae. That includes a lot of things that are . . . just creatures. Like animals. Here you have dogs and squirrels and bears. There they have raum and dennerlings and trow."

"And dragons?"

Bast shook his head. "Not that I've ever heard. Not any more."

Kostrel looked disappointed. "What about the fair folk? Like faerie tinkers and such?" He sat up stiffly, and quickly added. "Mind you, this isn't a *new* question. It's an attempt to focus your ongoing answer."

Bast laughed helplessly. "Lord and lady. *Ongoing*? Was your mother scared by an azzie when she was pregnant? Where do you get that kind of talk?"

"I stay awake in church," Kostrel said dryly. "And sometimes Abbe Leodin lets me read his books. What do the people who live there look like?"

"Mostly like regular people," Bast said simply.

"Like you and me?" the boy asked.

Bast fought back a smile. "*Just* like you or me. Odds are you wouldn't notice if they passed you on the street. But others? Some of them are . . . they're different. More powerful."

"Like Varsa Never-Dead or the Folding King?"

That brought Bast up short. "Where did you hear about the Folding King?" he asked without meaning to, his tone one of genuine surprise.

Kostrel grinned wickedly. "What will you give me for an answer to *that* question?"

Bast rubbed his face in disbelief, then he touched his forehead in a gesture that mimicked a formal bow despite the fact that he was sitting cross-legged in the grass with a wooly sheep embroidered on his pants.

"Some of the faen folk are like that," Bast conceded. "The way you hear in stories. Strength of arms, or charms, or tricks that put an Arcanist's to shame. But some are powerful in other ways. Like the mayor, or a moneylender." His expression went sour. "A lot of those types . . . they're not good to be around. They like to trick people. Play games with them."

Some of the excitement bled out of Kostrel at this. "Sounds like demons."

Bast started to shake his head, hesitated, then made a vague gesture instead. "Some are very much like demons," he admitted. "Or so close as makes no difference."

"Are some of them like angels, too?" the boy asked.

"It's nice to think that," Bast said. "I hope so. But my guess is most of them are more between than either-or."

"Where do they come from?"

Bast plucked a piece of grass and put it nonchalantly in his mouth. "That's your second question then?" he asked. "It must be, as it's got nothing to do with what the fae are *like*."

Kostrel grimaced, though Bast couldn't tell if he was embarrassed he'd gotten carried away, or ashamed he'd been caught out trying to get a free answer. "Is it true that faerie folk can never lie?"

"Some can't," Bast said. "Others simply find it ugly. Some lie but never break their word." He shrugged. "Others lie quite well, and do so every chance they get."

Kostrel opened his mouth, but Bast cleared his throat. "You have to admit," he said. "That's a pretty good first answer. I even gave you a few free questions."

"No you didn't," Kostrel said. "We agreed to three separate questions relating to a central topic. If you claimed a duplicate question was new, that would be bullshittery." He assumed a lofty expression. "It's more fair to say I generously assisted you in staying on-topic."

Bast chuckled low in his chest. "But you'll admit I've given a good answer, yes?"

Kostrel looked like he might argue for a second, then gave a slightly sullen nod. "What about my secrets then?"

"First," Bast held up a single finger. "Most of the fae don't come to this world. They don't like it. It rubs all rough against them, like a burlap shirt. But when they do come, they like some places better than others . . ." He trailed off playfully.

Kostrel's dark eyes were hungry and sharp as knives. Rather than resist being led, he charged ahead eagerly. "What places do they like?"

Bast felt his voice grow soft and slow. "First, I promised that I would be true, and to be clear, that's what I mean to do. So before I answer, I must say: there are uncounted varieties of fae. Many houses. Many courts. All colored in their subtle shades. All burning with their own strange fires. All ruled according to their own heart's desires. . . ."

He leaned forward and Kostrel unconsciously did the same. "Some have a tender love for nature's wild. Some are drawn to mortal hearth and home. Some find a secret place and stay, while others cannot help but roam."

Bast felt excitement rising in his chest, the rare bubbling delight that came from letting loose a hard-held secret that someone desperately desired. It was like candy, brandy, and a kiss together. "But something that appeals to all the fae are places with connections to the raw, true things that shape the world. Places that are touched with fire and water. Places that are close to air and stone. When all four come together. . . ." Bast's hands met between them, fingers interlacing.

Kostrel's face had lost all trace of its sharp cunning. He looked like a child again, mouth agape, his eyes wide and deep and soft with wonder.

Watching him, Bast felt joy like a needle strike clean through the center of his heart. Bast made an art of artifice, and he was justified in pride at all his clever craft. But this boy sat here being nothing but himself. His heart a harp that played no tune except his pure desire. It made Bast want to weep and howl. It made Bast wonder where he'd lost his way.

"Second secret." Bast raised a pair of slender fingers. "What I told you earlier was true. For the most part, faen folk look nearly like we do. But almost all of them have something to them that is slightly slant. Their smile. Their smell. The color of their eyes or skin. They might be just a bit too short, or thin. Perhaps a subtle shine when moonlight hits their hair. Another could be oddly strong or fair."

"Like Felurian!" Kostrel interjected.

"Yes, like Felurian," Bast said testily, thrown off his stride. "All those who walk the twisting roads between have charms to hide themselves, and more, as you're aware." He leaned back, nodding to himself. "That is a type of magic all the fair folk share."

Bast threw the final comment out like a fisherman casting a lure.

Kostrel swallowed hard. He didn't fight the line. He didn't even know that he'd been hooked. "That's my second question: What sort of magic can they do?"

Bast rolled his eyes dramatically. "Oh come now, that's another book's worth of question!"

"Well maybe you should just *write* a book then," Kostrel said sharply. "Then you can lend it to me and kill two birds with one stone."

The comment seemed to catch Bast by surprise. "Write a book?"

"That's what people do when they know every damn thing, isn't it?" Kostrel said sarcastically. "They write it down so they can show off."

"I'll give you the bones of what I know," Bast said. "First, the fae don't think of it as magic. They'll talk of art or craft. Seeming or shaping. But if they were to speak plainly, which they rarely do, they would call it glamourie and grammarie." Kostrel watched him, rapt, as Bast continued. "The twin arts of making something either *seem* or *be*."

Bast rolled on, caught up in the boy's excitement, his words coming fast and easy. "Glamourie is easier. With it they can make a thing seem other than it is. Make a white shirt seem like it is blue. Make a torn shirt seem like it is whole. Most folk have at least a scrap of glamour-art to hide their strangeness from a mortal's sight." Bast reached out to tug at a lock of Kostrel's hair. "Their glamourie could make gold hair look silver-white."

Kostrel's face was lost in wonder yet again. But . . . something was different now. Looking more closely, Bast saw it was no longer the gormless, gaping wonder of before. Now his eyes were sharp and glittering like knives. They showed a mind no longer dazzled by the *what*, and slowly moving to the point where they would ask a *how*.

Bast felt a chill run through him then. This is what came of letting down his guard. This is what happened when he let himself be bound, grounded, pulled so many ways. Why had he learned enough about the boy to feel fondness for him? It was like falling in love with a violet. It was like building a house on sand.

Feeling the cold sweat settle on him, Bast saw Kostrel's eyes as the wonder shifted slightly, became hungry, started to crystallize into questions such as, *'How do they make their glamour?'* and worse, *'How might a clever young boy break it?'*

And what would Bast do then, with a question like that hanging in the air? Break his promise fairly made? Here, where all things met? That was absolutely retrograde to his desire, and Bast could barely guess at what the consequence would be . . .

No. Far easier to tell the truth for now. Then make sure something happened to the boy. Something fast and final, unfortunate but clearly accidental. Sooner would be safer, too.

But . . . Bast liked this boy. He wasn't dull, or easy. He wasn't mean or low. He was foolish, fast, and hungry. Bast labored ages learning how to be a lamp, while this sweet child simply sat and shone like summer sun. The witty willful little tit was bright as broken glass and sharp enough to cut himself. And Bast too, apparently.

Bast rubbed his face. He had never been in conflict

with his own desire before this place. It used to be so easy. Want and have. See and take. Run and chase. Thirst and slake. Now everything was complicated. So much of what he longed for he could not pursue, and every day he felt more turned from his own true. . . .

"Bast?" Kostrel's head was cocked to the side. "Are you okay?" Awkward as a fawn, he reached out to put a hand on Bast's knee, patting it awkwardly, trying to comfort him.

No. Bast couldn't kill this boy. That would be too hard a thing.

Even so, Bast knew how fast a town could turn. He'd seen it. One day everything was kisses and cake, but let one little secret slip and suddenly the only choice was fire and iron, or flee and leave it all behind.

But here and now? He did not *want* to leave. What's more, his secrets were all tangled in his master's lies, so much he feared that one loose thread might cause the whole thing to unravel.

"You said grammarie was making something be?" Kostrel prompted gently.

Bast made an inarticulate gesture. He didn't have to feign a struggle. He'd promised honesty. He'd said too much. Killing this boy would be like shattering a stained glass window, but secrets would betray his master.

But saying nothing was the worst option. Bast knew how loud silence could be.

"Grammarie is . . . changing a thing," he said at last.

"Like turning lead into gold?" Kostrel asked, obviously trying to be helpful. "Is that how they make faerie gold?"

Bast made a point of smiling, though it felt stiff as leather on his face. "That's likely glamourie. It's easy, but it doesn't last. Fools who fall for faerie gold end up with pockets full of stones or acorns in the morning."

"But could they turn gravel into true gold?" Kostrel asked. "If they really wanted to?"

Bast felt the stiffness between his shoulders ease a bit. His smile softened, growing smooth. Of course. He was a curious boy. Of course. That was the narrow road between desires.

"It's not that sort of change," Bast said, though he nodded at the question. "That's too big. Grammarie is about . . . shifting. It's about making something into more of what it already is."

Kostrel's face twisted with confusion.

Bast took a deep breath and let it out through his nose. "I'm doing this wrong. What have you got in your pockets?"

Kostrel rummaged about and held out both his hands. There was a brass button, a piece of coal, a horse chestnut, a small folding knife . . . and a grey stone with a hole in it. Of course.

Bast slowly passed his hand over the collection of oddments, eventually stopping above the knife. It wasn't particularly fine, just a piece of smooth wood the size of a finger with a groove where a short, hinged blade was tucked away.

Bast picked it up delicately between two fingers. "What's this?"

"It's my knife," Kostrel said as he stuffed the rest of his belongings back into his pocket.

"That's it?" Bast asked.

"What else could it b—" The boy cut himself off before asking the full question, narrowing his eyes suspiciously. "It's just a knife."

Bast brought his own knife out of his pocket. It was a little larger, but instead of wood, it was carved from a piece of horn, polished and beautiful. When he opened it, the blade glittered sharp and white.

He lay both knives on the ground between them. "Would you trade your knife for mine?"

Kostrel eyed the knife jealously. But there wasn't a hint of hesitation before he shook his head.

"Why not?"

"Because it's mine," the boy said, his face clouding over.

"Mine's better," Bast said matter-of-factly.

Kostrel reached out and picked up his knife, closing his hand around it possessively. His face was sullen as a storm. "My da gave me this," he said. "Before he took the king's coin and went to be a soldier and save us from the rebels." He looked up at Bast, as if daring him to say a single word contrary to that.

Bast didn't look away from him, just nodded seriously. "So it's more than just a knife," he said. "It's special to you."

Still clutching the knife, Kostrel nodded, blinking rapidly.

"For you, it's the best knife."

Another nod.

"It's more important than other knives. And that's not just a *seeming*," Bast said, pointing. "It's something that knife *is*."

There was a flicker of understanding in Kostrel's eyes.

Bast nodded. "That's grammarie. Now imagine if someone could take a knife and make it be more of what a knife is. Make it the best knife. Not just for them, but for *anyone*." Bast picked up his own knife and closed it with a *clik*. "If they were truly skilled, they could do it with something other than a knife. They could make a fire that was more of what a fire is. Hungrier. Hotter. Someone truly powerful could do even more. They could take a shadow . . ." He trailed off gently, leaving an open space in the empty air.

Kostrel drew a breath and leapt to fill it with a question. "Like Felurian!" he said. "That's how she made Kvothe's shadow cloak?!"

Bast nodded seriously, glad for the question, hating that it had to be *that* question. "It seems likely to me. What does a shadow do? It conceals, it protects. Kvothe's cloak of shadows does the same, but more."

Kostrel was nodding along in understanding, and Bast pushed on quickly, eager to leave this particular subject behind. "Think of Felurian herself . . ."

Grinning, Kostrel seemed to have no trouble doing that.

"Someone beautiful," Bast said slowly, "can be a focus of desire. Felurian is that. Like the knife. The most beautiful. The focus of the most desire for everyone . . ." Bast let his statement trail off gently.

Kostrel's eyes were far away, obviously giving the matter his full deliberation. Bast gave him time for it, and after a moment another question bubbled out of the boy. "Couldn't it be merely glamourie?" he asked.

"Ah," said Bast, smiling wide. "But what is the difference between *being* beautiful and *seeming* beautiful?"

"Well . . ." Kostrel stalled for a moment, then rallied. "One is real and the other isn't." He sounded certain, but it wasn't reflected in his expression. "One would be fake. You could tell the difference, couldn't you?"

Bast let the question sail by. It was close, but not quite what he needed. "What's the difference between a shirt that *looks* white and a shirt that *is* white?" he countered.

"A person isn't the same as a shirt," Kostrel said with vast disdain. "If Felurian looked all soft and rosy like Emberlee, but her hair felt like a horse's tail, you'd know it wasn't real."

"Glamourie isn't just for fooling eyes," Bast said. "It's for everything. Faerie gold feels heavy. And a glamoured pig would smell like roses when you kissed it."

Kostrel reeled a bit, his imagination's shift from Emberlee to pig making him blink. "Wouldn't it be harder to glamour a pig?" he asked at last.

"You're clever," Bast said. "And you're exactly right. And glamouring a pretty girl to be *more* pretty wouldn't be much work at all. It's like putting icing on a cake."

Kostrel rubbed his cheek, his eyes focused on something far away. "Can you use both glamourie and grammarie at the same time?" he asked. "It seems like that would be the simplest way to get more penny for your pound of flour."

This startled Bast enough that his expression slipped. The boy was bright as freshly sharpened iron, and twice as dangerous to have so close to hand. Bast felt a warm pride glowing in his chest even as he felt a chill of fear at

what the boy might ask him next. Kostrel's third and final question waited like a tiger in the grass.

Bast nodded encouragingly. "I've heard that is the
way of things."

Kostrel looked thoughtful. "That's what Felurian must
do," he said. "Like cream on top of icing on a cake."

"I think so too," Bast said. "The one I met said s—"
He stopped abruptly, face a mask of startled fear as he
snapped his mouth shut. But it was obviously too late . . .

Kostrel's head snapped up suddenly, his eyes glittering with animal excitement. "You've met one of the Fae?"

Bast grinned. His perfect teeth were like a beartrap.
"Yes."

This time Kostrel felt both the hook and line, but far
too late. "You bastard!" he shouted furiously.

"I am," Bast admitted happily.

"You tricked me into asking that!"

"I did," Bast said. "It was a question related to this
subject, and I answered it fully and without equivo-
cation."

Kostrel got to his feet and stormed off, only to come
back a moment later, stomping heavily with his too-big
boots. "Give me my penny!" he demanded, holding out
his hand.

Bast pulled out a copper penny. "Where does Emberlee take her bath then?"

Kostrel glowered furiously, "After lunch on the Boggan farm," he said. "Out past Oldstone bridge, then up towards the hills about a quarter mile. A little sandy-bottom pool hidden by an ash tree."

Bast tossed him the penny, still grinning like mad.

"I hope your dick falls off," the boy said venomously before stomping back down the hill.

Bast couldn't help but laugh. But he did his best to do so quietly, as he liked Kostrel, and wanted to spare the boy's feelings. Even so, he didn't meet with much success, and the sound followed the freckled boy's retreat.

Kostrel turned at the bottom of the hill and shouted. "You still owe me a book!"

Bast stopped laughing as something jogged loose in his memory. Looking around, he panicked when he saw *Celum Tinture* wasn't in its proper spot.

Then he remembered leaving the book in the old holly tree and relaxed. The sky was clear, no sign of rain. It was safe enough.

He turned and hurried down the hill, not wanting to be late.

MID-DAY: BIRDS

BAST SPRINTED MOST of the way to the little dell, and by the time he arrived he was sweating like a hard-run horse. His shirt stuck to him unpleasantly, and as he walked down the sloping bank to the water he drew it over his head and used it to wipe the sweat from his face.

A long, flat jut of stone pushed out into Littlecreek there, forming one side of a calm pool where the stream turned back on itself. A stand of willows overhung the water, making it private and shady. The shoreline was overgrown with thick bushes, and the water was smooth and calm and clear.

Bare-chested, Bast walked out onto the rough jut of stone. When he was fully dressed, his face and long, dexterous hands made him look rather lean, but without his shirt, his shoulders were surprisingly muscled, more what you might expect to see on a fieldhand, rather than a shiftless sort that did little more than lounge around an empty inn all day.

Once he was out of the shadow of the willows, Bast knelt down to dunk his shirt in the pool. Then he wrung it over his head, shivering a bit at the chill of it. He rubbed his chest and arms briskly, shaking drops of water from his face.

He set the shirt aside, grabbed the lip of stone at the edge of the pool, then took a deep breath and dunked his head. The motion made the muscles across his back and shoulders flex. A moment later he pulled his head out, gasping slightly and shaking water from his hair.

Bast stood then, slicking back his hair with both hands. Water streamed down his chest, making runnels in the dark hair, trailing down across the flat plane of his stomach. He shook himself off a bit, then stepped over to a dark niche made by a jagged shelf of overhanging rock. He felt around for a moment before pulling out a knob of butter-colored soap.

He knelt at the edge of the water again, dunking his shirt several times, then scrubbing it with the soap. It took a while, as he had no washing board, and he obviously didn't want to chafe his shirt against the rough stones. He soaped and rinsed the shirt several times, wringing it out with his hands, making the muscles in his arms and shoulders tense and twine. He did a surprisingly thorough job, though by the time he was finished, he was completely soaked and spattered with lather.

Bast spread his shirt out on a sunny stone to dry. He started to undo his pants, then stopped and tipped his head on one side, tapping the heel of his hand against his temple, as if trying to jog water from his ear.

It might have been because of water in his ear that Bast didn't hear the excited twittering coming from the bushes that grew along the shore. It was a sound that could, conceivably, be sparrows chattering among the branches. A flock of sparrows. Several flocks, perhaps.

And if Bast didn't see the bushes moving either? Or note that in among the hanging branches of the willow

there were colors normally not found in trees? Sometimes a pale pink, sometimes a blushing red. Sometimes an ill-considered yellow or a cornflower blue. And while it's true that shirts and dresses might come in those colors . . . well . . . so did birds. Finches and jays. And besides, it was fairly common knowledge to the young men and women of the town that the dark young man who worked at the inn was woefully nearsighted and a bit of a fool besides.

So the birds tittered in the bushes as Bast worked at the drawstring of his pants again, the knot apparently giving him some trouble. He fumbled with it for a moment before he grew frustrated and gave a great, catlike stretch, his body bending like a bow.

Finally he managed to work the drawstring loose and shucked free of his pants. He wore nothing underneath, and when he tossed them aside there was a squawk from the willow of the sort that could have come from a larger bird. A heron perhaps. Or a crow. And if a branch shook violently at the same time, well, perhaps a bird had leaned too far from its branch and nearly fell. It certainly stood to reason some birds were more clumsy than others. Luckily, at the time, Bast was looking the other way.

Bast dove into the water then, splashing like a boy and gasping at the cold. After a few minutes he moved to

a shallower portion of the pool where the water rose to
barely reach his narrow waist.

Beneath the water, a careful observer might note
the young man's legs looked somewhat . . . odd. But it
was shady there, and everyone knows water bends light
strangely, making things look other than they are. And
besides, birds are not the most careful of observers, especially when there are other, more interesting places to focus their attention.

An hour or so later, slightly damp and smelling of sweet honeysuckle soap, Bast climbed the bluff where he was fairly certain he'd left his master's book. It was the third bluff he'd climbed in the last half hour, hunting for a particular tree.

When he reached the top, Bast relaxed at the sight of the holly. The branch and nook were right as he remembered, but the book was gone. A quick circle of the tree showed it hadn't fallen to the ground.

The wind stirred and Bast saw a white flicker like a tiny flag. He felt a sudden chill, fearing it might be a page torn loose. Few things angered his master like a mistreated book.

But no. Reaching up, Bast didn't feel the leather cover of the book that he expected, instead his fingers found a thick strip of birch bark held there with a stone. He pulled it down and saw the letters crudely scratched into the side.

I ned ta tawk ta ewe. Ets emportent.
Rike

I ned ta tawk ta ewe.
Ets emportent.
Rike

Bast had just made his way back to the lightning tree when he saw a young girl emerge into the clearing wearing a bright blue ruffled dress.

As she made her slow approach, Bast idly stirred the leather sack and made a pull. Looking down, he saw gold glittering against a flat black piece of slate. Lines of delicate engraving etched a chain into the stone. In the sunlight, it shone as bright as gilding.

The little girl didn't pause at the greystone, trudging straight past and up the side of the hill. She was younger than many of the children who came to the tree, perhaps six or seven. She wore fine slippers and had deep purple ribbons twining through her carefully curled hair.

Bast had never seen her before, but Newarre was a

small town. Even if he hadn't known her he could have guessed by her fine clothes and the smell of rosewater that this was Viette, the mayor's youngest daughter.

She climbed the low hill with grim determination, carrying something furry in the crook of her arm. When she reached the top of the hill she stopped and stood there, sweating a little and slightly fidgety, but still waiting.

Bast eyed her quietly for a moment, then slowly climbed to his feet. "Do you know the rules?" he asked seriously.

Viette stood, purple ribbons in her hair. She was obviously slightly scared, but her lower lip stuck out defiantly as she looked up at him. She nodded.

"What are they?"

The young girl licked her lips and began to recite in a singsong voice. "No one taller than the stone." She pointed to the fallen greystone at the foot of the hill. "Come to blacktree, come alone." She put her finger to her lips, miming a shushing noise. "Tell no—"

"Stop," Bast interrupted sharply, startling the girl a bit. "You say the last two lines while touching the tree."

The girl blanched a bit at this, but stepped forward and put her hand against the sun-bleached wood of the long-dead tree.

The girl cleared her throat again, then paused, her lips

moving silently as she ran through the beginning of the poem until she found her place again. "Tell no adult what's been said, lest the lightning strike you dead."

As she spoke the last word, Viette gasped and jerked her hand back, as if something had stung her. Her eyes went wide as she looked down at her fingertips and saw they were an untouched, healthy pink. Bast hid a smile behind his hand.

"Very well then," Bast said. "You know the rules. I keep your secrets and you keep mine. I can answer questions or help you solve a problem." He sat down again, his back against the tree, bringing him down to eye level with the girl. "What do you want?"

She held out the tiny puff of white fur she carried in the crook of her arm. It mewled. "Is this a magic kitten?" she asked.

Bast took the kitten in his hand and looked it over. It was a sleepy thing, almost entirely white. One eye was blue, the other green. "It is, actually," he said, sounding slightly surprised. "At least a little." He handed it back.

She nodded seriously. "I want to call her Princess Icing Bun."

Bast simply stared at her. "Okay," he said.

The girl scowled at him. "I don't know if it's a girl or a boy!"

"Oh," Bast said. He held out his hand, took the kitten, then petted it and handed it back. "It's a girl."

The mayor's daughter narrowed her eyes at him. "Are you fibbing?"

Bast blinked at the girl, then laughed. "Why would you believe me the first time and not the second?" he asked.

"I could *tell* she was a magic kitten," Viette said, rolling her eyes in exasperation. "I just wanted to make sure. But she's not wearing a dress. She doesn't have any ribbons or bows. How can you tell if she's a girl?"

Bast opened his mouth. Then closed it again. This was not some farmer's child. She had a governess and a closet full of clothes. She didn't spend her days around pigs and goats. She'd never seen a lamb born. It was an easy question. What wouldn't be easy was an angry mayor storming through the front door of the Waystone, demanding why his daughter suddenly knew the word 'penis.'

Still, it was simple enough to answer. Bast would rather tell the bigger truth than the smaller one anyway. "Bows and dresses don't matter much," he said. "She decided she's a girl, so she's a girl."

Viette looked at him suspiciously. "But how do *you* know what she decided?" Her eyes widened. "Can you talk to kittens?"

"I can," Bast said smugly.

The little girl's eyes went wide, and she visibly swelled with excitement. She drew in a breath, then paused and let it out slowly. "They said you were sly . . . ."

"I am," Bast admitted.

"Anyone can talk to kittens, can't they?"

Bast grinned at the girl. He'd have to watch this one. In a couple years she'd give Kostrel a run for his money. "They can if they want to."

"What I *mean*," she said, emphasizing the word, "is do kittens talk to *you*?" Then she quickly added, "So's you can understand them?"

"No," Bast said. Then amended his answer to be perfectly honest. "Hardly ever."

She scowled furiously. "So how do you know she decided to be a girl?"

He hesitated. He'd rather not lie. Not here. But he hadn't promised to answer her question, hadn't made any sort of agreement at all with her, in fact. That made things easier.

"I tickle the kitten's tummy," Bast said. "And if it winks at me, I know it's a girl."

This seemed to satisfy Viette, and she nodded gravely. "How can I get my father to let me keep it?"

"You've already asked nicely?"

She nodded. "Daddy hates cats."

"Screamed and thrown a fit?"

She rolled her eyes and gave an exasperated sigh. "I've *tried* all that, or I wouldn't be here."

Bast thought for a moment. "Okay. First, get some food that will keep good for a couple days. Biscuits. Apples. Nothing with a strong smell. Hide it in your room where nobody will find it. Not even your governess. Not even the maid. Do you have a place like that?"

The little girl nodded.

"Then go ask your daddy one more time. Be gentle and polite. If he still says no, don't be angry. Just tell him you love the kitten. Say if you can't have her, you're afraid you'll be so sad you'll die."

"He'll still say no," the little girl said matter-of-factly.

Bast shrugged. "Probably. But here's the second part. Tonight, pick at your dinner. Don't eat it. Not even the dessert." The little girl started to say something, but Bast held up a finger to stop her. "If anyone asks, just say you're not hungry. Don't mention the kitten. When you're alone in your room tonight, eat some of the food you've hidden."

The little girl looked thoughtful.

Bast continued. "Tomorrow, don't get out of bed. Say you're too tired. Don't eat your breakfast. Don't eat your lunch. You can drink a little water, but just sips. Just lay in bed. When they ask what's the matter—"

She brightened. "I say I want my kitten!"

Bast shook his head, his expression grim. "No. That will spoil it. Just say you're tired. If they leave you alone, you can eat, but be careful. If they catch you, you'll never get your kitten."

The girl was listening intently now, her brow furrowed in concentration.

"By dinner they'll be worried. They'll offer you more food. Your favorites. Keep saying you're not hungry. You're just tired. Just lay there. Don't talk. Do that all day long."

"Can I get up to pee?"

Bast nodded. "But remember to act tired. No playing. The next day, they'll be scared. They'll bring in a doctor. They'll try to feed you broth. They'll try everything. At some point your father will be there, and he'll ask you what's the matter." Bast grinned. "That's when you start to cry. No howling. Don't blubber. Just tears. Can you do that?"

"Yes."

Bast raised an eyebrow.

The little girl rolled her eyes and gave an exasperated sigh ten years too old for her. Then she stared Bast right in the face, blinked, blinked again, and suddenly her eyes welled up with tears until they spilled over and ran down her cheeks.

As an artist, Bast admired natural talent when he saw it. He clapped expansively, his face solemn as a judge.

Viette dipped a tiny curtsey in return, crisp as a fencer's salute. "I didn't even show you the lip . . ." she said.

"I'm sure it's devastating," Bast said without a hint of mockery, then continued. "So you lay there. Just the tears.

Don't say anything until your father comes and asks. Then you say you miss your kitten. Remember you're supposed to be weak. You haven't eaten in days. Just the tears and you say you miss your kitten so much you don't want to be alive any more."

The little girl thought about it for a long minute, petting the kitten absentmindedly with one hand. Finally she nodded, "Okay." She turned to go.

"Hold on now!" Bast said quickly. "I gave you two answers and a way to get your kitten. You owe me three things."

The little girl turned around, her expression an odd mix of surprise and embarrassment. "I didn't bring any money," she said, not meeting his eye.

"Not money," Bast said. "You pay with favors, labors, secrets. . . ."

She thought for a moment. "Daddy hides his strong-box key inside the mantle clock."

Bast nodded approvingly. "That's one."

The little girl looked up into the sky, still petting her kitten. "I saw mama kissing the maid once."

Bast raised an eyebrow briefly at that. "That's two."

The girl put her finger in her ear and wiggled it. "That's all, I think."

"How about a favor, then?" Bast said. "I need you to fetch me two dozen daisies with long stems. And a blue ribbon. And two armfuls of gemlings."

Viette's face puckered in confusion. "What's a gemling?"

"Flowers," Bast said, looking puzzled himself. "Maybe you call them balsams? They grow wild all over around here," he said, making a wide gesture with both hands.

"Do you mean geraniums?" she asked.

Bast shook his head. "No. They've got loose petals, and they're about this big." He made a circle with his thumb and middle finger. "They're yellow and orange and red. . . ."

The girl stared at him blankly.

"Widow Creel keeps them in her window-box," Bast continued. "When you touch the seed pods, they pop."

Viette's face lit up. "Oh! You mean *touch-me-nots*," she said, her tone more than slightly patronizing. "I can bring you a bunch of those. That's *easy*." She turned to run down the hill.

Bast called out before she'd taken six steps. "Wait!" When she spun around, he asked her, "What do you say if somebody asks you who you're picking flowers for?" She rolled her eyes again. "I tell them it's none of their tupping business," she said imperiously. "Because my daddy is the mayor."

••••◉••••

After Viette left, Bast lay back against the grass of the hill and closed his eyes. He'd barely been dozing for a quarter hour when a high whistle pierced the air. It wasn't loud, but the sound of it made Bast sit bolt upright as quickly as if it had been a scream.

The whistle came again, and Bast found himself on his feet like a puppet with a string tied round its heart. He fought the urge to run like a dog called to dinner, and instead forced himself to stretch and roll his neck, running his fingers through his still-damp hair.

Looking down from the top of the hill, Bast didn't see any children waiting by the greystone. He cast about a bit, and for someone as nearsighted as he was supposed to be, he didn't seem to have any trouble picking out the slim figure standing in the shadows of the trees two hundred feet away.

Bast sauntered down the hill, across the grassy field, and under the gently shifting shadows of the wood. An older boy stood there. His lean face was sharp and smudgy, softened a little by a boyishly pug nose. He was barefoot, with ragged hair, and as Bast came close he shifted his weight with the anxious energy of a stray dog, half-bristling with defiance, half-ready to run.

"Rike." Bast's voice held none of the friendly, bantering tone he'd used with the town's other children. "How's the road to Tinuë?"

"A long damn way from here," the boy said bitterly, not meeting Bast's eye. "We live in the ass of nowhere."

"I see you have my book," Bast said.

The boy held it out, causing the cuff of his shirt to slide up, revealing more thin, smudgy arm. "I wann't tryin' to steal it," he muttered quickly. "I just needed to talk to you."

Bast looked down at the book, scowling. But while he was almost certainly a fool, he was not the sort to worry over a penny's worth of thread. The sun seemed to go behind a cloud for a moment as Bast took hold of the book, then frowned when he felt the weight of it.

"I din't break the rules," Rike said quickly, his eyes still on the ground. "I din't even come into the clearing. But I need help. And I'll pay."

Bast wanted to refuse. Instead he said, "You lied to me, Rike."

"And din't I pay for that?" the boy demanded, anger threading through his sullen voice. "Din't I pay for it ten times? En't my life shit enough without having more shit piled on top?"

"And we both know you're too old," Bast said grimly.

"I aren't either!" The boy stomped a foot, then clenched his jaw and took a deep breath, visibly struggling to keep his temper. "Tam is a year older'n me and he can still come to the tree! I'm just taller'n him!"

"It's not my fault you broke the rules, boy," Bast said, and while his face didn't change, there was a thread of menace woven through his voice.

Rike's head snapped up then, his eyes burning. "I en't your boy!" he snarled, his anger tearing out of him. "And it en't my fault your rules are shite!" Rike's voice was thick with scorn, "I don't know why I even bother with you!"

Rike jabbed his finger angrily at Bast, shouting so savagely his teeth showed. "Everyone knows you en't worth a tinker's damn!" Rike's eyes were wide and wild as a dog with the froth, so furious they were almost blind as he continued, "You're a worthless little bastard, and you deserve more of the belt than you get!"

There was a long silence broken only by the boy's ragged breathing. Rike's eyes were fixed on the ground again, his fists clenched at his sides. He was shaking.

Bast's eyes narrowed ever so slightly.

"Jus—" The boy's voice broke, and he swallowed hard. He tried again. "Just one." Rike's voice was rough, as if he'd hurt it shouting. "Just one favor. Just this once. I'll pay anything. I'll pay triple."

Rike unclenched his fists with an obvious effort. He was still shaking, but all the anger was gone. "Just . . . please?"

Eyes still on the ground, Rike took a hesitant half-step forward. His hand reached out and hung there aimlessly, then the boy timidly caught hold of Bast's shirtsleeve, tugging it once before letting his hand fall back to his side. His voice was thin as a broken reed. "Please, Bast?"

At the sound of Rike speaking his name, Bast felt himself sweat cold. He felt weak as wet paper. Like his lungs were full of water. Like his bones were cold iron. Like the sun had gone black in the sky.

Then everything came rushing back. Bast put one hand against a nearby tree. He could feel the rough flake of pine bark on his fingertips. He gasped for breath and realized he was already breathing. He took a half-step away from the boy, just out of arm's reach . . . and was surprised his legs were capable of supporting his weight.

Rike looked up, eyes full of tears. His face was twisted in a knot of anger and fear. A boy too young to keep from crying, but still old enough so he couldn't help but hate himself for doing it. "I just can't fix this on my own."

Bast drew a deep breath, then let it out again. "Rike . . ."

"I need you to get rid of my da," the boy said in a broken voice. "I can't figure a way. I could stick him while he's asleep, but my ma would find out. He drinks and hits at her. And she cries all the time and then it's worse."

Bast stood very still. Perfectly still, as if he were about to flinch.

But Rike was looking at the ground again, words

pouring out of him in a gush. "I could get him when he's drunk somewhere, but he's so big. I couldn't move him after. They'd find the body and the azzie would come get me. I couldn't look my ma in the eye then. Not if she knew. I can't think what that would do to her, if she knew I was the sort of person that would kill his own da."

He looked up then, his eyes furious and red with weeping. When he spoke, his voice was flat and cold. "I would though. I'd kill him. I just need your help."

There was a moment of silence between them no longer than a breath.

"Okay," Bast said.

NOON: OBLIGATION

RIKE NEEDED A moment to collect himself, or at least that's what Bast assumed. What the boy had actually said was that he needed to see a man about a horse, before dashing off into the shrubbery.

Bast sighed like a child in church and peered up at the sun. The turning wheels of his desire did not come grinding to a halt because some farmer drank too much. He already had enough to do today. Emberlee would be taking her bath soon. He needed carrots for the stew . . .

But his unresolved debt to the boy was like a thorn straight through his tongue. And that was when Rike was elsewhere. Close at hand, it was more like a razor, freshly stropped and pressed against his throat. The fact that the boy didn't know his hand was on the handle wasn't at all reassuring.

And as if the situation wasn't tangled tight enough, the boy had broken faith with Bast before. That was no little thing.

Before coming to this place with his master, Bast would have reveled in the boy's betrayal. Revenge was such a simple, raw desire. Satisfying, clean as fire. There was a sort of dark, hard joy that came from settling a score so solidly it burned some mortal's life straight down to ash.

Instead, for the first time, Bast found he wasn't free to do such things. Or rather, he was free to choose between desires. To take the sweet and terrible revenge that he was due . . . or continue to assist his master. To keep their masks intact and stay here tucked away inside the new-built inn, all hidden in this quiet little town.

And so, last summer, Bast chose to thwart his own desire, an act as natural as pulling out his tongue. And yes, he had still paid Rike back for his betrayal. And yes, he'd wrought revenge all cunning, coy, and cruel. But still, for

Bast it was like craving steak and getting gruel. It was like slaking want of wine by licking at its shadow on a wall.

And this, apparently, was Bast's reward for showing such remarkable restraint and moving counter to his natural desires: the boy he'd spared now had him on a leash.

But the favor Rike was asking for . . . it might be a bit of hidden luck. If Bast stepped quickly enough, there was a chance he could slip loose before disaster struck. It had been a near thing in the woods just now.

Sighing again, Bast looked around aimlessly until Rike came out of the brush lacing up his pants. Wordlessly, he turned and led the boy out of the wood, into the clearing, back toward the hill.

Bast walked as far as the greystone. There were no children waiting, so he stopped and turned to Rike. "Tell me exactly what you want," he said, leaning against the side of the great sun-warmed stone. "Do you want to kill him? Or do you just want to have him gone?"

Eyes still red around the edges, Rike hunched under the question, putting his hands in his pockets. "He went gone a whole two span about a year ago." The faint ghost of a smile flickered on the boy's smudged face. "That was a good time, just me and Ma and Tess. It was like my birthday every day when I woke up and he weren't there. I never knew my ma could sing. . . ."

The boy went quiet again. "I thought he'd fallen somewhere drunk and finally broke his neck." The smile was gone now. Rike rubbed his eyes, then spat into the grass. "Turns out he'd just traded off a mess of furs for drinking money. He'd been off in his trapping shack, all stupor-drunk for half a month."

Rike took his hands out of his pockets, then didn't seem to know what to do with them and put them back. He shook his head. "No. If he was just gone, I'd never sleep again for worry he'd come back." Rike was quiet for a bit. "No," he said, more firmly this time. "No. If he goes I know that he won't stay away."

"I can figure out the how," Bast said. "You need to tell me what you really want."

"It needs done soon," Rike said, a thread of bone-deep panic underneath his voice. "How much a difference does that make?"

Looking up at the sun, Bast sighed. Some things could not be easily ignored.

And yet, some things could not be easily forgot.

Turned against himself, Bast brought out the leather sack and pulled an embril. Holding it in his fist, he wordlessly tilted the open sack toward the boy.

Rike looked puzzled, but after a brief rummage, he brought out his hand and showed the piece of slate etched with a chain. There was no gold this time, only the silver-grey of iron.

Bast opened his hand, revealing a rough disk of obsidian. Its surface had no image at all. But one edge was chipped, and as they both looked down, they saw the blood well up all of a sudden in a bright red line where it had cut Bast's palm.

Scowling, Bast gave a disgusted snort and rolled his eyes as if the world had just told him a long-winded, unfunny joke. He held out the sack ungraciously, then shook it impatiently after half a moment when Rike failed to immediately drop the piece of slate inside.

After Rike did, Bast returned the embrils to his pocket and looked the boy in the eye. "What's your father's name?"

"Jessom," Rike said, his face looking like he was tasting something bitter.

"Assuming we can come to an agreement. Assuming soon. Which is it? You want him dead or gone?"

Rike stood there for a long while, jaw clenching and unclenching. "Gone," he said at last. The word seemed to catch in his throat. "So long as he stays gone forever. If you can really do it."

"I can do it," Bast said calmly.

Rike looked at Bast, then back down at his hands. "Gone then," he said at last. "I'd kill him. But that sort of thing en't right. I don't want to be that sort of man. A fellow shouldn't ought to kill his da."

"I could do it for you," Bast said easily, as if they were trading chores. "No blood on your hands then."

Rike sat for a while, then shook his head. "It's the same thing, innit? Either way it's me. And if it were me, it would be more honest if I did it with my hands, rather than do it with my mouth."

Bast shrugged easily. "Right then. Gone forever?"

"Gone forever," Rike said, then swallowed hard. "And what's this going to cost?"

"A lot," Bast said. "It won't be buns and buttons, either. Think how much you want this. Think how big it is." He met the lean boy's eyes and didn't look away. "That much three times over. That's what you'll owe. Plus some on top for *soon*." He stared at the boy. "Think hard on that."

Rike was a little paler now, but his eyes were flint, and his mouth made a line. "Anything," he said. "But nothin of Ma's. She en't got much left that Da hasn't drank away."

Bast looked the boy up and down. "You're mine until I say we're square. Secrets. Favors. Anything." Bast gave him a hard look. "That's the deal."

Rike had gone even paler than before, but he nodded. "So long as it's only me. None of Ma's or anything that touches her. And it *has* to be soon," Rike said. "He's getting worse. I can run off, but Ma can't. And little Bip can't neither. And . . ."

"Fine fine," Bast cut him off testily, waving his hands. "And yes, soon."

Bast turned, circled round the greystone, then started to make his way up the side of the hill, motioning for

Rike to follow. They climbed for a minute in silence. The sun went behind a cloud, making the mild summer day turn suddenly chill and grey.

Bast crested the hill with Rike in tow for the first time in more than a year. Together they moved to stand beside the stark white trunk of the lightning tree. The wind kicked up a bit, tossing Bast's black hair as the sun came out from behind the cloud, making everything glow warm with the buttery light.

Bast held up his hand, palm bright with blood. He pressed it hard against the barkless trunk. Underhand, he tossed the piece of chipped obsidian to Rike.

Rike caught the embril easily, and without hesitation cut a line beneath his four fingers. The blood welled up and Rike stepped closer, pressing his hand against the warm, smooth wood.

The two of them stood there, one tall, one short. Each standing on their own side with their arms outstretched, it looked like they were holding up the broken tree.

Bast met the boy's eyes. "You want to strike a deal with me?"

Rike nodded.

"Say it then," Bast said.

Rike said, "I want to make a deal."

Bast gave the barest shake of his head. "Say: *'Bast, I want you to make a deal with me.'*"

Rike drew a breath before he continued. "Bast," he said, with such deadly earnest solemnity that a priest would envy it. "Please make a deal with me."

Rike watched as Bast bowed his head slightly. The tall man's body shuddered slightly, as if suddenly shouldering some impossibly heavy weight.

Bast drew a breath and straightened. His careful steps described a circle round the tree, but somehow he still stayed right where he stood. Rike blinked, as if he wasn't sure what he had seen.

Bast spun, the motion like a dancer's leaping twirl, but somehow he still stood and kept one hand against the broken trunk beside him. Rike blinked, then blinked again. The place where Bast was standing wavered, rippling like a flat road on a blazing summer day.

Bast carefully did not make a gentle circle with his hand and fought the urge to grin. Every day he made this place his own. He wove it strong. He wore it thin.

Bast drew a deep, unfettered breath and felt the edges of the world begin to slip and fold. There was the smell of torn and burning wood. The sun flickered in the sky. The shadow underneath the vast and spreading branches of the oak was dark as night. The stars were out.

Bast smiled as underneath the weight of his desire, time began to shift and break. The air was still. His eyes were dark and terrible. Then, graceful as a dancer, he lifted up his leg to take a step . . .

••••◦◉◦••••

. . . and Bast came to the top of the hill with Rike for the first time that day. Again. They came there for the first time and again. And together they walked to stand beside the bare trunk of the lightning tree. The sun was warm as honey. The wind bent the tall grass to lick against their legs.

Bast turned to look Rike in the eye and nodded seriously.

"Help me get my da to go away," Rike said. "Forever. So my ma don't ever have to see him even once again."

Bast pressed his bloody palm against the pristine whiteness of the tree. "Gone forever," he agreed. "And soon."

"You do this favor for me," Rike said. "I'll owe you. I'll work f—"

"No." Bast's voice was like a bar of lead. He tossed the piece of sharp obsidian to Rike, red sunset glittering like blood along its broken edge. "I do this and you're *mine* 'til I say otherwise."

Rike swallowed hard. "I swear it." He sliced his palm below the thumb. The white trunk of the lightning tree was shaded red with sunset as he pressed his bloody hand against it. "You make him go so far away his shadow never lays across a road where my ma has to set her feet."

⚬⚬⚬◆⚬⚬⚬

Bast led Rike to take their places by the lightning tree, for the first time and again. The wind brushed cool against them, drying the sweat from their foreheads. Bast's skin seemed paler in the fading light, as if reflecting the light of the hanging crescent moon.

Rike staggered slightly, catching himself with one hand against the side of the lightning tree. He could feel the wetness there tug slightly as the cool, dry wood soaked up his blood.

Bast pressed his hand against the pale side of the tree. "I do this, and I own you to the middle of your bones." His eyes were the same perfect purple of the fading twilight sky behind him. "I ask you for your thumb? You run to find a boning knife. You have a sweet dream late at night, you wrap it in a bow and bring it right to me."

"I swear it." Rike shivered in the chill night air. He cut his hand. His hand was pressed against the tree. Bast handed him the embril, and he caught it. "Make it so he goes and won't come back." Rike licked his lips. "But leave him living, even though my heart wants him to die."

$\cdots\bullet\bullet\bullet\bullet\cdots$

Rike crested the hill for the first time in more than a year to find Bast waiting for him, standing in the dark beside the lightning tree. The wind was sharp, the embril that he held felt colder than a chip of ice. The moon hung straight above them, sharp and bright.

Rike pricked his fingers one at a time. His hand seemed impossibly white in the moonlight. Each drop of blood was perfectly black.

"She never has to look at him again," Rike said. "Tess never has to hide when she hears boots outside the door. Little Bip will never have to learn his name. Gone until every one of us forgets his face forever, even when we dream." He touched his fingers to the tree and felt them freeze and stick and burn, like when he touched the pump handle on the coldest days in winter.

"I do this, and I will never owe you any other thing," Bast said, his empty eyes glittering like the stars scattered across the perfect blackness of the sky above. "Any debt or obligation will be squared. Any gifting that you've made to me is all unbound and now instead becomes a freely given gift, offered without obligation, let, or lien."

"You do this and we're square," Rike said. "Anything you say I do. But nothing against my ma, or Tess, or little Bip. I only owe what's mine, and that's the deal."

Bast reached up and gently ran his palm along the sharp white knife edge of the moon and pressed it to the nearby tree. "Gone forever, still alive, and soon. I swear it on my blood and name. I swear it by the ever-moving moon." Bast's skin seemed almost to shine in the dark. "Here in this place, between the stone and sky, I swear to you three times and done."

Rike pulled away from the tree. He held out a hand as if trying to catch his balance, but his body didn't sway unsteadily. He didn't feel dizzy either, though he did close his eyes and take a deep breath while resting his hands on the warm surface of the greystone where he sat.

Bast licked the blood from his palm, watching Rike

like a cat. The sun came out from behind a cloud, warming both of them while the wind made waves whisper through the tall grass.

Rike swung his feet a couple times idly, then made the short hop down from sitting on the greystone to land lightly on the grassy ground. "So. Where do we start?"

"First, let me see your hands," Bast said.

"Why?" Rike asked, puzzled.

Bast tilted his head the barest fraction of an inch and gave the boy a look of perfect, pure, impassive calm.

Rike blanched and stepped forward instantly, holding out both hands. Bast reached out gingerly, first touching the back of the boy's hand with a single finger. Nothing. He took gentle hold of Rike's wrist next. Then seeming to gain confidence, Bast took hold of both hands and turned them palm-side up. They were smudged as if the boy had been climbing rocks or trees. There were a few scuffs and old scars, but that was all.

Seeming satisfied, Bast let go of the boy's hands and they fell loose back to his sides. Bast fought the urge to wipe his own hands on his pants. "Second, find Kostrel," he said instead. "Tell him I have some of what I owe him."

For half a second, it seemed like Rike might say something. Then he simply bobbed his head once.

Bast gave a wicked smile at this and nodded his approval. "Third time is the charm," Bast pointed at the stream. "Go find a river stone with a hole clean through it. Then bring it here to me."

"A faerie stone?" Rike blurted.

Bast needed to nip that in the bud. "Faerie stone?" he said in a tone so scathing Rike flushed red. "You're too old for nonsense." Bast gave the boy a look. "Do you want my help or not?" he asked.

"I do," Rike said in a small voice.

"Then bring me a river stone." Bast pointed imperiously off in the direction of the nearby stream. "You have to be the one to find it, too," he improvised. "Can't be anyone else. Can't be traded for. And you need to gather it the proper way so we can use it for the charm: dry on the bank where the sun has touched it, hole pointed up at the sky."

Rike nodded.

Bast struck his hands together sharply once. It sounded like a tiny thunderclap. Rike went racing like a hound after a hare.

Laying back in the grass, Bast plucked a stem of grass and chewed it. He rubbed his chest idly, delighting in the lightness there. True, he had a bargain he was bound to

104

honor. And Rike had been insistent upon 'soon,' and Bast had sworn, so it needed tending to today. And yes, he already had plans, and this was going to complicate them . . .

But who didn't enjoy a bit of a challenge every now and then? And if he had a little extra on his plate, what better day than Midsummer for fitting extra in? Bast would have paid ten times the price to be out from under the boy's thumb. Fifty times. He smiled like a cat who knows which window in the creamery is loose. There was still work ahead, but as an artist, Bast felt a certain satisfaction with what he'd begun.

AFTERNOON: STILL

WITH NO CHILDREN waiting, Bast skipped stones in the nearby stream. He snuck up on a frog and startled it. He flipped through *Celum Tinture*, glancing at the illustrations: Calcification. Titration. Sublimation. He pulled a pair of embrils, then spent a long while puzzling at the pairing of the Empty Scales and the Winter Tree.

Brann, happily unbirched with a well-bandaged hand, brought him two sweet maple buns wrapped in a fine white handkerchief. Bast ate the first and set the second to one side.

Viette brought armloads of flowers and a fine blue ribbon. Bast wove the daisies into a crown, incorporating the ribbon so it ran twisting through the stems in an elaborate braided pattern.

Finally, looking up at the sun, Bast saw it was nearly time. He removed his shirt and filled it with the wealth of red and yellow touch-me-nots. He added the handkerchief and crown, then fetched a stick and made a bindle so he could carry the lot without the risk of crushing them.

He headed past the Oldstone Bridge, then up toward the hills and around a bluff until he found the place Kostrel had described. It was tucked tidily away. The stream curved and eddied into a lovely little pool perfect for a private bath.

Bast walked upstream, peering intently at the water as he went. He was forced to detour around a piece of boggy ground, then an outcrop of stone, then came upon an absolutely impenetrable patch of wild raspberry that forced him to turn back. He headed downstream to the Oldstone Bridge, then crossed the stream and headed back, exploring the other bank.

He met with fewer obstacles this time, and was able to stay much closer to the stream. He eyed the water closely, tossing in a leaf, a piece of bark, a handful of grass. He peered up at the sun. He listened to the wind. He scurried up and down the bank a dozen times.

Eventually he either learned what he set out to, or simply became bored. Returning to the secluded shaded pool, he hunkered down behind some bushes and was almost nodding off until the crackle of a twig and a scrap of song snapped him sharply awake. Peering down, he saw a young woman making her careful way down the steep hillside to the water's edge.

Silently, Bast scurried upstream with his bundle. Three minutes later he was kneeling on a piece of grassy waterside where he had left the bright pile of flowers.

He picked up a yellow blossom, held it close, and when his breath brushed the petals, its color changed into a delicate blue. He dropped it in the water, watching as the current slowly carried it away.

Bast gathered up a handful of posies, red and orange, and breathed on them again. They too changed until they were a pale and vibrant blue. He scattered them onto the surface of the stream. He did this three more times until there were no flowers left.

Then, picking up the handkerchief and daisy crown, he sprinted back downstream, across the bridge, then around and over to the cozy little hollow with overarching elm.

He'd moved so quickly that Emberlee was just arriving at the water's edge.

Softly, silently, he crept up to the spreading elm. Even with one hand carrying the handkerchief and crown, he went up the side as nimbly as a squirrel.

Soon Bast lay along a low branch, sheltered by leaves, breathing fast but not hard. Emberlee was removing her stockings and laying them carefully on a nearby hedge. Her hair was a burnished golden red, falling in lazy curls. Her face was sweet and round, a lovely shade of pale and pink.

Bast grinned as he watched her look around, first left, then right. Then she began to unlace her bodice. Her dress was a cornflower blue, edged with yellow, and when she spread it on the hedge, it flared and splayed like the wing of a bird. Perhaps some fantastic combination of a finch and a jay.

Dressed only in her shift, Emberlee looked around again: left, then right. Then she shimmied free of it, a fascinating motion. She tossed the shift aside and stood there, naked as the moon. Her creamy skin was amazing with freckle. Her hips wide and delightful. The tips of her breasts were brushed with palest of pink.

She scampered into the water, making a series of small,

dismayed cries at the chill of it. They were, on consideration, not really similar to a crow's at all. Though they could, perhaps, be slightly like a heron's.

Emberlee washed a bit, splashing and shivering. She ran a cake of soap between her hands, then soaped herself. She dunked her head and came up gasping. Wet, her curling hair clung to her, the color of ripe cherries.

That was when the first of the blue touch-me-nots arrived, drifting on the water. She glanced at it curiously as it floated by, then began to lather soap into her hair.

More flowers followed. They came downstream and spun circles around her, caught in the slow eddy of the pool. She looked at them, amazed. Then sieved a handful from the water and brought them to her face, drawing a deep breath to smell them.

She laughed delightedly and dunked under the surface, coming up in the middle of the flowers. The water sluiced her pale skin, but the blossoms clung to her, tangling in her hair and pressing to her skin as if reluctant to let go.

That was when Bast fell out of the tree.

There was a brief, mad scrabbling of fingers against bark, a bit of a yelp, then he hit the ground like a sack of suet. He lay on his back in the grass and let out a low, miserable groan.

He heard a splashing, and then Emberlee appeared above him. She held her white shift in front of her. Bast looked up from where he lay in the tall grass.

He'd been lucky to land on that patch of springy turf. A few feet to one side, and he'd have broken hard against the rocks. Five feet the other way and he would've ended wallowing in mud.

Emberlee knelt beside him, her skin pale, her hair dark. One posy clung to her neck. It was the same color as her eyes, a pale and vibrant blue.

"Oh," Bast said happily as he gazed up at her. His eyes were slightly dazed. "You're so much lovelier than I had hoped."

Emberlee rolled her eyes, but still favored him with a fond smile.

He lifted a hand as if to brush her cheek, only to find it holding the crown and knotted handkerchief. "Ahh," he said, remembering. "I've brought you some daisies too. And a sweet bun!"

"Thank you," she said, taking the daisy crown with both hands. She had to let go of her shift to do this. It fell lightly to the grass.

Bast blinked, momentarily at a loss for words.

Emberlee tilted her head to look at the crown. The

ribbon was a striking blue, but it was nothing near as lovely as her eyes. She lifted it with both hands and set it proudly on her head. Her arms still raised, she looked down at Bast and drew a long deliberate breath.

Bast's eyes slipped from her crown.

She smiled at him indulgently.

Bast drew a breath to speak, then stopped and drew another through his nose. Honeysuckle.

"Did you steal my soap?" he asked incredulously.

Laughing happily, Emberlee bent to kiss him.

••••◦◉◦••••

Bast made a wide loop up into the hills north of town. It was wild and rocky up that way. No soil deep or flat enough to plant, the ground too treacherous for grazing.

Even with the boy's directions, it was hard to find Martin's still. He had to give the crazy bastard credit, between the brambles, rockslides, and fallen trees, Bast never would have found it accidentally. What at first looked like a willow brake turned out to be the entrance to a scrubby little box valley. At the back of the valley was an overhang above a shallow cave with three quarters of a shack built out of it.

Bast slowed as soon as he saw the front door of the shack. He had some small experience sneaking in and out of places folk wanted to keep private. As such, he knew a hundred simple, vicious tricks used to discourage the overly curious.

Bast found excitement bubbling up in him as he began to slowly search for whatever Martin had set up to guard his still. Most folks showed reasonable restraint, knowing the people mostly likely snooping were neighbors. It was one thing to set a trap that might leave someone scratched or limping so you could tell who'd been nosing in your secrets. But you still needed to live in the community, so there were limits to what most folk would do.

But Martin wasn't known for restraint, or even pleasantness, much less a desire to be a peaceful part of the community. Bast knew this better than anyone, as less than a minute after he'd first met the huge man, Martin had thrown a hatchet straight at his head before charging in, both fists swinging, shouting something about demons and barley. Bast would have liked to hear everything more clearly, but he'd been busy running through the trees like a rabbit with a hot coal up its ass.

After asking around a bit, Bast discovered that while this was extreme, it wasn't out of character for the great bear of a man. He was widely regarded as the best distiller and poacher in town, hobbies he pursued openly, with a flagrant disregard for the king's law.

But despite the fact that he sold his meat cheap and fletched the best arrows in town, Bast quickly learned what folk appreciated most about Martin was that the wild-eyed man came to town infrequently, and kept those visits brief.

So Bast found himself grinning as he swept his gaze around the shack. He could hardly guess what sort of safeguards a true maniac like Martin would devise to keep his precious secrets safe.

But half an hour of careful searching later, Bast hadn't found a thing. No stumble-wire to drop a bank of stone down where the path went narrowly between two rocks. No fishhooks dipped in piss and hung face-high, hidden in the branches. No deadfalls. No crossbows. No jaw-traps. Nothing. Bast didn't find as much as a string of bells or a shallow hole covered in old leaves.

Confused and disappointed, Bast wasn't hoping for much when he finally entered the shack. But opening the door, he found himself surprised a second time.

The inside was as tight and tidy a little space as Bast had ever seen. Dried flowers and herbs hung in bundles from the rafters. A rug of woven grass covered the floor.

The still wasn't some slipshod contraption bunged together out of old pots and pine pitch either. It was a work of art.

A great covered copper kettle twice the size of a washbasin dominated the back of the shack, emerging from a huge, well-mortared fieldstone smoulder-stove. A wooden trough ran all along the ceiling, and only after following it outside did Bast realize it was for bringing in rainwater, and could be diverted into several different channels or used to fill the cooling barrels.

There were basins and buckets, a large screw press and a set of smaller presses using stones. Lines of bright copper tubing crossed the room, some passing through a collection of makeshift glass containers on a high shelf that looked like they held flowers, brightly colored fruit, and other things Bast could only guess at.

Eyeing the twists and spirals of copper running between the barrels and bottles and basins, Bast had the sudden urge to flip through *Celum Tinture* and learn what all the different pieces of the still were called. What they were for. Only then did he realize he'd left the book somewhere again . . .

So instead, Bast rooted around until he found a box filled with a mad miscellany of containers. Two dozen bottles of all sorts, clay jugs, old canning jars. . . . A dozen of them were full. None of them were labeled in any way.

Bast lifted out a tall glass bottle that he guessed had once held wine. He pulled the cork, sniffed, then took a careful sip. His face bloomed into a sunrise of delight. Despite the fact that this place reminded him of his master's workshop, Bast had half-expected it to taste of char and turpentine.

But this was . . . well . . . he wasn't sure entirely. He took another drink. There was something of apples about it. Some spice? It smelled ever so slightly of cinnas fruit and violets, and . . . honey?

Bast took a third drink, grinning. Whatever you cared to call it, it was lovely. Smooth and strong and just a little sweet. Unseen, Bast lifted the bottle in a toast to the absent master of the still. Martin might be mad as a badger, but he obviously knew his liquor.

⋯⋯⦿⋯⋯

It was better than an hour before Bast managed to make it back to the lightning tree. *Celum Tinture* was there, having slid off a smooth rock to lay in the grass, apparently unharmed. For the first time he could remember, Bast was glad to see the book. He flipped it open to the chapter on distillation and read for half an hour, nodding to himself at various points, flipping back to look at diagrams and illustrations. Turns out the thing was called a condensate coil. He'd thought it looked important. And expensive, being made entirely of copper.

Eventually he closed the book and sighed. There were a few clouds rolling in, so no good could come of leaving the book unattended. His luck wouldn't last forever, and he shuddered to think what would happen if the wind tumbled the book into the grass and tore the pages. Or if there was a sudden rain. . . .

So Bast wandered back to the Waystone Inn and slipped through the back door. Stepping carefully, he made his way into the taproom, opened a low cupboard, and tucked the book inside. He made his silent way halfway back to the stairs before he heard footsteps behind him.

"Ah, Bast," the innkeeper said nonchalantly. "Have you brought the carrots?"

Bast froze, caught awkwardly mid-sneak. He straightened up and brushed self-consciously at his clothes. "I . . . I haven't quite got round to that yet, Reshi."

The innkeeper gave a deep sigh. "Bast, I don't ask a . . ." He stopped and sniffed, then eyed the dark-haired man narrowly. "Are you drunk?"

Bast looked affronted. "Reshi!"

The innkeeper rolled his eyes. "Fine then, have you been drinking?"

"I've been *investigating*," Bast said, emphasizing the word. "Did you know Crazy Martin runs a still?"

"I'd heard," the innkeeper said, his tone making it clear he didn't find this information to be particularly thrilling. "And Martin isn't crazy. He just has a handful of unfortunately strong affect compulsions. And a touch of tabard madness from when he was a soldier, unless I miss my guess."

"Well, yes . . ." Bast said slowly. "I know, because he set his dog on me and when I climbed a tree to get away, he tried to chop the tree down. And also set fire to the tree. And then he went to get his bow. But also, aside from those things, he's crazy too, Reshi. Really, really crazy."

"Bast," the innkeeper said reproachfully, giving him a chiding look.

"I'm not saying he's *bad*, Reshi. I'm not even saying I don't like him. But trust me. I know crazy. His head isn't put together like a normal person's."

The innkeeper gave an agreeable if slightly exasperated nod. "Noted."

Bast opened his mouth, then looked slightly confused. "What were we talking about?"

"Your advanced state of investigation," the innkeeper said, glancing out the window. "Despite the fact that it is barely past noon."

"It's Midsummer, Reshi," Bast said plaintively, as if that explained everything.

The innkeeper merely blinked at him, his expression not changing.

Bast rolled his eyes. "You know how early it gets light on Midsummer, Reshi? Today is twice as long as some days we get in the winter." As he continued, the innkeeper's incurious stare seemed to erode Bast's surety, but he pushed on. "What I'm saying is that if it were winter right now, Reshi. I mean, if today were *in* winter then it would already practically be evening by now." He hesitated. "With how early I got up, I mean."

The innkeeper was quiet for a long moment. Then he drew a deep breath and continued in a level tone. "If that stunning logical syllogism isn't proof of your sobriety, I don't know what is, Bast. Notwithstanding . . ."

"Oh, yes!" Bast said excitedly. "I know Martin's been running a tab, and I know you've had trouble settling up because he doesn't have any money."

"He doesn't *use* money," the innkeeper corrected gently.

"Same difference, Reshi," Bast sighed. "And it doesn't change the fact that we don't need another sack of barley. The pantry is choking on barley. But since he runs a still . . ."

The innkeeper was already shaking his head. "No, Bast," he said. "I won't go poisoning my customers with hillwine. You have no idea what can end up in that stuff."

"But I *do* know, Reshi," Bast said. "Ethel acetates and methans. And tinleach. There's none of that."

The innkeeper blinked. "Did . . . ?" He stopped. Started again. "Bast, have you actually been reading *Celum Tinture*?"

"I did, Reshi! For the betterment of my education!" Bast beamed proudly. "And my desire to not poison our customers or go blind my own self. I got a taste, and I can say with confident authority that what Martin makes is far away from hillwine. It's lovely stuff. Halfway to Rhis, and that's not something I say lightly."

The innkeeper stroked his upper lip thoughtfully. "Where did you get some to taste?" he asked.

"I traded for it," Bast said, deftly skirting the edges of the truth. "Not only would it give Martin a chance to settle his tab, but it would help us get new stock in. I know that's harder these days, roads bad as they are . . ."

The innkeeper held up both hands helplessly. "I'm already convinced, Bast."

Bast grinned happily.

"Honestly," the innkeeper said, "I would have done it for the sole reason of celebrating you reading your lesson for once. But it will be nice for Martin, too. It will give him an excuse to stop by more often. It will be good for him."

Bast's smile faded a bit.

If the innkeeper noticed, he didn't comment on it. "I'll send a boy round to Martin's and ask him to come by with a couple bottles."

"Get a dozen if he has them," Bast said. "Or more. It's getting cold at night. Winter's coming, and what he's got will be like drinking a piece of spring while sitting round the fire."

The innkeeper smiled. "I'm sure Martin will be flattered by your glowing recommendation."

Bast paled, his expression showing raw dismay. "By all the gorse *no*, Reshi," he said, waving his hands frantically in front of himself. "Don't tell him *I* said anything. Don't even tell him I plan on drinking it. He hates me."

The innkeeper hid a smile behind his hand.

"It's not funny, Reshi," Bast said angrily. "He throws rocks at me!"

"Not for months," the innkeeper pointed out. "Martin

has been perfectly cordial to you the last several times he's stopped by for a visit."

"Because there aren't any rocks inside the inn," Bast said.

"Be fair, Bast," the innkeeper continued chidingly. "He's been civil for almost half a year. Polite even. Remember he apologized to you two months back? Have you heard of Martin ever apologizing to anyone else in town? Ever?"

"No," Bast said sulkily.

The innkeeper nodded. "See? That's a big gesture for him."

"I'm sure he's turning a new leaf," Bast muttered. "But if he's here when I get home, I'm eating dinner on the roof."

••••◆••••

Bast was restless as he lay back on the grass beside the lightning tree. He shifted, stood, and went to get a drink from the stream that wound around the bottom of the hill. Coming back to the top, he circled the tall, white broken tree. Back and forth, winding and unwinding.

He sat again, uncomfortably, like a cat that's been

rubbed backwards. He felt around inside himself, and found what he knew would be true. The only obligations binding him were old, familiar things. Most barely more than scars. Some few resembling wounds old soldiers had. A shoulder that grew stiff with cold. A knee that ached when rain was on the way.

But nothing new. It was galling, as he'd been pleased how tidily he'd slid from underneath the unexpected dangers of the day. So why then did he feel more turned against himself than ever? Rucked up and tugged a dozen ways.

Finally he pulled out the leather sack. He stilled himself, closed his eyes, and pulled a full fist of embrils, tossing them up with a fluid, flippant grace.

He heard them hit the earth like hail, and opened his eyes to study them: a crescent of white horn, an oval of dark wood laying partly on top of the painted piper dancing on a piece of glazed white tile. There was a candle etched into an oblong stone, a disc of clay, the flat green stone he'd traded from the baker's boy. There was the galling sun-bright bit of brass, and once again the one that very much looked like an old iron coin.

Soon the sound of Kostrel and his too-big boots came up the hill to stand beside him. The boy folded his arms and tried to look cross, but he wasn't good at it. His features were too friendly. While he was clearly trying for a scowl, his freckled face just barely held a frown.

Not bothering to look up at the boy, Bast held out a small book bound in deep green leather. When the boy reached out and took it with both hands, Bast felt the faintest thread of debt pull loose inside him.

Kostrel opened the book and flipped some pages. "Looks like herbs or something?"

Bast shrugged, continuing to stare pensively at the scattering of embrils on the ground.

Kostrel's attempt at petulance faded, and his expression returned to its more natural curiosity. "So . . ." he said casually. "Did you manage to catch Emberlee?"

This pulled Bast's attention away from the stones, and he looked up at the boy.

"I did," Bast said slowly, eyes still fixed carefully on Kostrel's face. He saw it there again, something sitting not quite right. Not fear, or even nervousness. Those were too big, and would be obvious as a burr on his cuff. This was more like a grain of sand down the collar of his shirt.

Kostrel saw him staring and looked away.

It clicked into place then. Bast's mouth went open in shock and admiration. "You didn't find it," he said. "She told you!"

"What? Who?" Kostrel's expression was shocked and innocent, and while he made a good showing, it was still a mistake. Bast had been playing that game longer than the boy had been alive.

To his credit, Kostrel knew he'd been caught out, and immediately abandoned the act. "I got you though," he said, eyes glittering with joy. His expression far more innocent than any he might try to feign.

Bast shook his head, blinking with genuine surprise. "You did an amazing job selling it," he said. "I hope you turned a profit, too. What did Emberlee charge you for her bathing spot?"

Kostrel gave Bast a puzzled look. "Why would I buy it?" he said. "She wanted me to pass it off to you. She owed *me* a favor for that."

Twice in as many minutes, Bast was shocked into silence.

Kostrel laughed at him. "Oh come *on*," he said, rolling his eyes a bit. "You lot think you're *so* sly and secret, but you're not."

Bast looked genuinely offended. "I'll have you know," he said with affronted dignity, "that I am, in fact, quite sly. And secret as well."

Kostrel sighed a bit, and shrugged as if conceding a point. "You're decent," he said. "And Emberlee plays a good game too. But Kholi doesn't have a lick of shame. And Dax—" Kostrel paused a moment, as if reconsidering his words. "Dax has many good qualities that make him ideally suited to sitting and watching sheep all day."

"He has more good qualities than that," Bast said, smiling a wide smile.

Kostrel rolled his eyes again. "I *know* he does. Because Kholi tells *everyone*. But he also blushes red as a slapped ass when anyone teases him." The boy shook his head. "I swear, the lot of you hopping in and out of haystacks like rabbits, hiding in bushes. Everyone knows. Everyone with at least one eye and half a brain in their head."

Bast blinked, then tilted his head curiously. "What favor did you ask Emberlee for?"

"A gentleman doesn't tell," Kostrel said with airy dignity, then gave a grin somehow more innocent and wicked than any Bast had ever seen.

Knowing better than to lock horns with Kostrel when he was even slightly spun, Bast went to get a drink from the stream and splash a little water on his face.

As he collected himself, he was surprised to realize he didn't mind losing a round to Kostrel. In fact, it filled him with an odd delight. It had been years since he'd been completely taken in, and any game grows boring if you always win. So he would need to dance a little faster if he wanted to keep Kostrel on his toes. And Emberlee as well, it seemed.

When Bast came back to the top of the hill, Kostrel was staring at the scattering of embrils. "My granda has a Telgim set," the boy said. "He used to throw stones to tell him the best time to plant. Drove my gran crazy." He leaned forward to look more closely. "What'd you ask 'em?"

"Nothing," Bast said, sitting down again. But here, beside the tree, the near-lie prickled him. "There's only one question anyone is ever truly interested in," he amended. "What now?"

The boy nodded, looking down. "You get anything?"

Bast turned his head to see Kostrel eyeing the embrils so fiercely it was almost comical. A smile began to flicker on Bast's face. "How would you read it?"

Kostrel folded to the ground in the boneless way that children have. "I don't know the proper names for all of them," he admitted. "My granda only showed me a bit, and mostly when he'd had a few nips and wanted to rile up Gran."

"Names are fine," Bast said, shrugging with one shoulder. "But if you know what something's called, it's hard to keep wondering what it is." He gestured. "The embrils aren't like names that pin things to a page. Their nature is to twist and change. They remind us that the world is vast and deep. They teach us of the distance between catch and keep."

Kostrel smiled. "That sounds like my granda. He says reading them keeps a mind from getting stiff, like old leather that hasn't been oiled." He leaned forward. "Show me how you'd read it first."

Bast sighed, sounding stuck between frustration and exhaustion. "We've got the moon." He touched the crescent of white horn. He moved his finger to the green stone with the woman's face. "Then here's a woman sleeping. And here's the lamp unlit. So it's night? A woman is sleep-

ing at night?" He shook his head. "That's a long walk for not much road."

"Here's the piper." Bast pointed to a painted figure on the white tile, a drum strapped to his hip. "He's overlapped by the closed eye. So he's asleep too?" He flicked his fingers at the teardrop of the penance piece. "The burning tower signifies ruin and destruction . . . but it's shaped like a drop, so . . . water? Maybe rain?"

"Then there's the candle and the stone arch," Bast said. "If they were next to each other, it could mean a journey. If the woman's sleeping, it might be a dream . . ."

Kostrel pointed to the piece of jagged metal that very much looked like an iron coin. "What about that one, with the crown?"

Bast shrugged, but not as casually as before. Perhaps his mouth drew slightly tight as well. He was about to dismiss the question, but seeing the boy's eyes, Bast remembered silence was the worst option with Kostrel. If Bast didn't give him something, the boy would fixate on this like a bit of gristle stuck between his teeth.

"Iron crown is authority or rule," Bast said, trying to sound bored. "But marred I'd read it as domination." He paused, then decided he might as well make a clean breast of it. "By itself, it signifies the Shattered King. Majesty and power, but in ruin. Fallen into despair."

"Despair?" Kostrel asked, puzzled.

Bast blinked and shook his head, genuinely irritated. "No," he said. "I meant disrepair." He bulled ahead quickly, gesturing at the entire spread. "It's a mess. Parts of it fit together, but . . ." He threw his hands into the air and let them fall again, exasperated. "It doesn't really *say* anything."

"That's not how I'd read it at all . . ." Kostrel said hesitantly.

Bast made a welcoming gesture. "Please."

Kostrel touched the green stone gently with one finger. "This is a moss agate. Moss is soft and delicate, but agate is a hard, hard stone." He slid the broken crown above the face carved into the green stone. "She's a queen."

He scooted forward so his shorter arms could reach the embrils. "I don't think she's sleeping, either." He slid the brass coin closer. "This isn't rain. It's a tear. She's soft but hard. Powerful and sad. Her tower is broken." He made a sweeping gesture. "She's the Weeping Queen."

He pointed at the piece of horn showing the crescent moon. "I don't know about that. Maybe it's not even the moon? Maybe it's a bowl? Or horns? Since it's so thin, maybe it means something is about to end? Like when the moon has almost gone away?"

Kostrel's tone grew more confident as he continued. "The piper isn't sleeping either." He touched the clay disk. "The lamp is his. A lamp is what you use to find your way, or read at night. Unlit? That means the piper's in the dark. That means he's lost, or ignorant."

The boy brought his finger back to the piper. "The closed eye? He's blind. He's supposed to play for folk, make them dance to his tune. But *he's* the one dancing." Kostrel was caught up enough that he laughed at this. "He's dancing but he's too blind to even know it!"

He pointed. "The candle isn't lit either. So . . . is he three times blind? Or . . . wasted potential? Fire that's waiting?" Kostrel trailed off, tapping his lips.

Bast was looking at the embrils more intently now. "What about the arch?" he asked, something odd in his tone.

Kostrel didn't seem to notice. "I dunno about that. It's canted, so . . . maybe it's supposed to be a hole the piper might fall into?" The boy thought a moment longer, then shrugged and rubbed his nose. "My granda used to say you shouldn't work too hard to make all the pieces fit.

When he did a bigger read, he said there was always one pull you needed to ignore. Half of reading proper was figuring out which one."

Bast reached out, grinning suddenly as he tousled Kostrel's hair. Then without any preamble, he gathered up his embrils and was down the hillside fast as dancing, heading off, far and away.

•••••••

Bast had been trotting briskly for a quarter mile when he finally heard Rike calling his name through the trees. Surprised, Bast slowed to a stop and watched the boy run up the thin dirt path toward him.

"I've got it!" Rike said triumphantly. Breathless, he held up his hand. The entire lower half of his body was dripping wet.

"What, already?" Bast asked.

The boy nodded and flourished the dark stone between two fingers. It was flat and smooth and rounded, slightly smaller than the lid of a jam jar. "What now?"

Bast stroked his chin for a moment, as if trying to remember. "Well . . . now we need a needle. But it has to be borrowed from a house where no men live."

Rike looked thoughtful for a moment, then brightened. "I can get one from Aunt Sellie!"

Bast fought the urge to curse. He'd forgotten Sellie's older child had declared they didn't care to be called Mikka any more. They were Grett now, and had been drinking harthan tea. "Oh, two women in the house is certainly *adequate* . . ." Bast lightly gilded the word with disdain. ". . . if that's all you want. But the charm will be stronger if the needle comes from a house with a *lot* of women living in it. The more the better."

Rike looked up for another moment, searching his memory. "Widow Creel has two daughters . . ." he mused.

"Dob's living there too now," Bast pointed out. "A house where no men *or boys* live."

"But where a lot of girls live . . ." Rike stood there, dripping, slowly running through the options in his head. Finally he brightened. "Old Nan!" he said. "She don't like me none. But I reckon she'd give me a pin."

"A needle," Bast stressed. "And you have to borrow it." Bast watched the boys eyes narrow, and quickly added. "She has to lend it to you. You steal it, or try to buy it off her, it won't work for the charm." He raised an eyebrow at the boy. "Also, I hope it goes without saying that you can't tell her what you truly need the needle for."

"I can't tell what I don't know," Rike groused, but only very softly.

Bast half expected the boy to follow up with questions about the particulars of the charm Bast had been hinting at. Or that he might complain about the fact Old Nan lived all the way off on the other side of town, about as far southwest as you could go and still be considered part of Newarre. It would take the boy half an hour to get there, and even then, Old Nan might not be home.

But Rike didn't so much as sigh. He just nodded seriously, turned, and took off at a sprint, bare feet flying as he headed to the southern end of the king's road.

Nodding to himself, Bast continued in the direction he'd been heading, off to the northern outskirts of the town. . . .

MOONRISE: SWEETNESS

SURE THAT RIKE would be busy for at least an hour, Bast took his time. He hopped a fence to cut through the Forsens' fields. He climbed a tree and found a pine cone that he liked. He ignored a cat. He chased a squirrel. He found an old well covered by a dozen badly rotting planks.

The Williams farm wasn't a farm in any proper sense, not for a long while at any rate. The fields had been fallow so long, it was hard to see that they had ever been plowed at all, overrun with brambles and spotted with sapling trees. The tall barn had fallen into disrepair, and half the roof gaped open, a dark hole against the clear blue sky.

Walking up the long path through the fields, Bast turned a corner and saw Rike's house. It told a different story than the barn. It was small but tidy. The shingles needed some repair, but otherwise it looked well tended-to. Yellow curtains were blowing out the kitchen window, and the flower-box was spilling over with fox fiddle and marigold.

There was a pen with a trio of goats on one side of the house. On the other side was a large garden. The fence was not much more than lashed-together sticks, but Bast could see straight lines of flourishing greenery inside. Carrots. He still needed carrots.

Craning his neck a bit, Bast saw several large, odd shapes behind the house. He took a few more steps to the side and eyed them before he realized they were beehives.

Just then there was a storm of barking and two great, floppy-eared black dogs came bounding from the house toward Bast, baying for all they were worth. When they came close enough, Bast got down on one knee and wrestled with them playfully, scratching their ears and the ruffs of their necks.

After a few minutes of this, Bast continued to the

house, the dogs weaving back and forth in front of him before they spotted some sort of animal and tore off into the underbrush. He knocked politely at the front door, though after all the barking his presence could hardly be a surprise.

The door opened a couple inches, and for a moment all Bast could see was a slender slice of darkness. Then the door opened a little wider, revealing Rike's mother. She was tall, and her curling brown hair was springing loose from the braid that hung down her back.

She swung the door fully open, holding a tiny, half-naked baby in the curve of her arm. Its round face was pressed into her breast and it was sucking busily, making small grunting noises.

Glancing down, Bast smiled happily at the baby. She followed his gaze down and stared fondly at her nursing child for a moment, too. Then she looked back up to favor Bast with a warm smile. "Hello Bast, what can I do for you?"

"Ah. Well," he said. "I was wondering, ma'am. That is, Mrs. Williams—"

"Nettie is fine, Bast," she said indulgently. With the notable exception of Crazy Martin, most of the townsfolk found Bast pleasant enough, though most of them also considered him somewhat simple in the head, a fact Bast didn't mind in the least.

"Nettie," Bast said, smiling his most ingratiating smile.

There was a pause, and she leaned against the door-frame. A little girl peeked out from around the woman's faded blue skirt, nothing more than a pair of serious dark eyes.

Bast smiled at the girl, who disappeared back behind her mother.

Nettie looked at Bast expectantly. Finally she prompted, "You were wondering . . . ?"

"Oh, yes," Bast said. "I was wondering if your husband happened to be about."

"I'm afraid not," she said. "Jessom's off checking his traps."

"Ah," Bast said, disappointed. "Will he be back any time soon? I'd be happy to wait."

She shook her head, "I'm sorry. Odds are he'll do his lines, and spend tonight skinning and drying up in his shack." She nodded vaguely toward the northern hills.

"Ah," Bast said again.

Nestled snugly in her mother's arm, the baby drew a deep breath, then sighed it out blissfully, going quiet and limp. Nettie looked down, then up at Bast, holding a finger to her lips.

Bast nodded and stepped back from the doorway as Nettie stepped inside, deftly detached the sleeping baby from her nipple with her free hand, and carefully tucked the child into a small wooden cradle on the floor. The dark-eyed girl emerged from behind her mother and went to peer down at the baby, hands clasped behind her back.

"Call me if she starts to fuss," Nettie said softly. The little girl nodded seriously, sat down on a nearby chair, and began to gently rock the cradle with her foot.

Nettie stepped outside, closing the door behind her. She walked the few steps necessary to join Bast, rearranging her bodice unselfconsciously. In the sunlight Bast noticed her high cheekbones and generous mouth. Even so, she looked more tired than anything, her dark eyes heavy with worry.

The tall woman crossed her arms over her chest. "What's the trouble then?" she asked wearily.

Bast looked confused. "No trouble," he said. "I was wondering if your husband had any work."

Nettie uncrossed her arms, looking surprised. "Oh."

"There isn't much for me to do at the inn," Bast said

a little sheepishly. "I thought your husband might need an extra hand . . . ."

Nettie looked around, eyes brushing over the old barn. Her mouth tugging down at the corners. "He traps and hunts for the most part these days," she said. "Keeps him busy, but not so much that he'd need help, I imagine." She looked back to Bast. "At least he's never made mention of wanting any."

"How about yourself?" Bast asked, giving his most charming smile. "Is there anything around the place you could use a hand with?"

Nettie smiled at Bast. It was only a small smile, but it stripped ten years and half a world of worry off her face, making her practically shine. "There isn't much to do," she said apologetically. "Only three goats, and my boy minds them."

"Firewood?" Bast asked. "I'm not afraid to work up a sweat. And it has to be hard getting by with your gentleman gone for days on end." He grinned at her hopefully.

"And we just haven't got the money for help, I'm afraid," Nettie said.

"I'm supposed to get carrots," Bast said cheerfully.

Nettie looked at him for a minute, then burst out laughing. "Carrots," she said, rubbing at her face. "How many carrots?"

"Maybe . . . six?" Bast asked, not sounding very sure of his answer at all. "Is six a good number of carrots?"

She laughed again, shaking her head a little. "Okay. You can split some wood." She pointed to the chopping block that stood in back of the house. "I'll come get you when you've done six carrot's worth."

Bast set to work eagerly, and soon the yard was full of the crisp, healthy sound of splitting wood. The sun was still strong in the sky, and after a few minutes Bast was covered in a sheen of sweat. He carelessly peeled away his shirt and hung it on the nearby garden fence.

Leaving aside the fact that most folk in the town would be surprised to see him doing any sort of work at all, there wasn't anything particularly odd about how Bast went about the chore. He split wood the same way everyone did: you set the log upright, you swung the axe, you hit the wood. There wasn't room in the experience to extemporize.

Even so, there was something in the way he went about the task that caught the eye. When he set the log upright, he moved intently. Then he would stand for a small moment, absolutely still. Then came the swing. It was a fluid thing. The placement of his feet, the play of the long muscles in his arms. . . .

There was nothing exaggerated. Nothing like a flourish. Even so, when he brought the axe up and over in a perfect arc, there was a grace to it. The sharp cough the wood made as it split, the sudden way the halves went tumbling to the ground. He made it all look somehow . . . *dashing.*

He worked a hard half hour, at which time Nettie came out of the house, carrying a glass of water and a handful of fat carrots with the loose greens still attached. "I'm sure that's at least a half a dozen carrots' worth of work," she said, smiling at him.

Bast took the glass of water, drank half, then bent and poured the rest over his head and the back of his neck. He shook himself off a bit, then stood back up, his dark hair curling and clinging to his face. "Are you sure there's nothing else you could use a hand with?" he asked, giving

her an easy grin. His eyes were dark and smiling and bluer than the sky.

Nettie shook her head. When she looked down, loose curls of dark hair fell partly across her face. "I can't think of anything," she said.

"I'm a dab hand with honey, too," Bast said, hoisting the axe to rest against his naked shoulder.

She looked a little puzzled at that until Bast nodded toward the mismatched hives scattered across the overgrown field. "Oh," she said, as if remembering a half-forgotten dream. "I used to do candles and honey. But we lost a few hives to that bad winter three years back. Then one to nits. Then there was that wet spring and three more went down with the chalk before we even knew." She shrugged. "Early this summer we sold one to the Hestles so we'd have money for the levy. . . ."

She shook her head again, as if she'd been daydreaming. She shrugged and turned back to look at Bast. "Do you know about bees?"

"A fair bit," Bast said softly. "They aren't hard to handle. They just need patience and gentleness." He casually swung the axe so it stuck in the nearby stump. "They're the same as everything else, really. They just want to know they're safe."

Nettie was looking out at the field, nodding along with Bast's words unconsciously. "There's only the two left," she said. "Enough for a few candles. A little honey. Not much. Hardly worth the bother, really."

"Oh come now," Bast said gently. "A little sweetness is all any of us have sometimes. It's always worth it. Even if it takes some work."

Nettie turned to look at him. She met his eyes now. Not speaking, but not looking away either. Her eyes were like an open door.

Bast smiled, gentle and patient, his voice was warm and sweet. He held out his hand. "Come with me," he said. "I have something to show you."

EVENING: RIDDLES

THE MIDSUMMER SUN was slowly making its way toward the horizon, but still hung high in the sky as Bast came back to the clearing. He was limping slightly and had dirt in his hair, but he seemed in good spirits.

There were two children at the bottom of the hill, sitting on the greystone and swinging their feet as if it were a huge stone bench. Bast didn't even have time to sit down before they came up the hill together.

It was Wilk, a serious boy of ten with shaggy blonde hair. Behind him was his little sister Pem, half his age with three times the mouth.

The boy nodded at Bast as he came to the top of the hill, then he looked down. "You okay?"

Glancing down, Bast was surprised to see a few dark streaks of blood dripping from his hand. He brought out his handkerchief and daubed at his knuckles as elegantly as a duchess brushing away crumbs at dinner.

"How did your hand get hurt?" little Pem asked him.

"I was attacked by four bears," Bast lied breezily.

The boy nodded agreeably, giving no indication of whether or not he believed Bast. "I need a riddle that will stump Tessa," the boy said. "A good one."

"You smell like granda," Pem chirruped as she came to stand beside her brother.

Wilk ignored her. Bast did the same.

"Okay," said Bast. "I need a favor, I'll trade you. A favor for a riddle."

"You smell like granda when he's been at his medicine," Pem clarified brightly.

"It has to be a good one though," Wilk stressed. "A real stumper."

"Show me something that's never been seen before and will never be seen again," Bast said.

"Hmmm . . ." Wilk said, looking thoughtful.

"Granda says he feels loads better with his medicine,"

Pem said louder, plainly irritated at being ignored. "But mum says it's not medicine. She says he's on the bottle. And granda says he feels loads better so it's medicine by dammit." She looked back and forth between Bast and Wilk, as if waiting for them to scold her.

Neither of them did. She looked a little crestfallen.

"That is a good one," Wilk admitted at last. "What's the answer?"

Bast gave a slow grin. "What will you trade me for it?"

Wilk cocked his head on one side. "I already said. A favor."

"I traded you the riddle for a favor," Bast said easily. "But now you're asking for the answer. . . ."

Wilk looked confused for half a moment, then his face went red and angry. He drew a deep breath as if he were going to shout. Then seemed to think better of it and stormed down the hill, stomping his feet.

His sister watched him go, then turned back to Bast. "Your shirt is ripped," she said disapprovingly. "And you've skint your knuckles and got grass stain on your pants. Your mam is going to give you a hiding."

"No she won't," Bast said smugly. "Because I'm all grown, and I can do whatever I want."

"Can't neither," Pem said.

"Can so," Bast riposted. "I could light my pants on fire, and I wouldn't get in any trouble at all."

The little girl stared at him with smoldering envy.

"And every night for dinner I get to eat a whole cake," Bast added.

Wilk stomped back up the hill. "Fine," he said sullenly.

"My favor first," Bast said. He handed the boy a small bottle with a cork in the top. "I need you to fill this up with water that's been caught midair."

"What?" Wilk said.

"Naturally falling water," Bast said. "You can't dip it out of a barrel or a stream. You have to catch it while it's still in the air."

"Water falls out of a pump when you pump it . . ." Wilk said without any real hope in his voice.

"*Naturally* falling water," Bast said again, stressing the first word. "It's no good if someone just stands on a chair and pours it out of a bucket."

"What do you need it for?" Pem asked in her little piping voice.

"And what will you trade me for the answer to that question?" Bast said.

The little girl went pale and slapped both hands across her mouth.

"It might not rain for *days*," Wilk said.

Pem let her hands fall away and gave a gusty sigh. "It doesn't have to be rain," his sister said, her voice dripping with condescension. "You could just go to the waterfall by Littlecliff and fill the bottle there."

Wilk blinked.

Bast grinned at her. "You're a clever girl."

She rolled her eyes, "Everybody says that . . ."

Bast brought out something from his pocket and held

157

it up. It was a green cornhusk wrapped around a daub of sticky honeycomb. The little girl's eyes lit up when she saw it.

"I also need twenty-one perfect acorns," he said. "No holes, with all their little hats intact. If you gather them for me over by the waterfall, I'll give you this."

She nodded eagerly. Then both she and her brother hurried down the hill.

••••◉◉••••

Bast went back down to the pool by the spreading willow and took another bath. It wasn't his usual bathing time, so there were no birds waiting. Because of this and the fact that Emberlee still had his soap, the entire affair was much less elaborate this time. He rinsed himself clean of sweat and honey, then daubed a bit at his clothes as well, scrubbing to get rid of the grass stains and the smell of lavender and cinnas fruit. The cold water stung the cuts on his knuckles a bit, but they were nothing serious and would mend well enough on their own.

Naked and dripping, he pulled himself from the pool and found a dark rock, hot from the long day of sun. He draped his clothes over it and let them bake dry while he shook his hair out and stripped the water from his arms and chest with his hands.

Then he lay down on the rock himself, spreading across the smooth warm surface like a cat. An impressive bruise was flowering on his thigh, with a matching one near his ribs. But they didn't seem to trouble Bast overmuch. Folding his arm behind his head to make a pillow, he closed his eyes and nodded off, undressed and unconcerned, face peaceful in the fading light.

SUNSET: LIES

SHADOWS STRETCHED TO cover Bast, and he shivered himself awake. He sat up, rubbing his face and looking around blearily. The sun was just flirting with the tops of the western trees.

After dressing in his now-dry clothes, he made his way back to the lightning tree. Wilk and Pem hadn't returned, but that was hardly a surprise. He ate the piece of honeycomb he'd promised Pem, licking his fingers. Then he chewed the wax idly as he watched a pair of hawks turn lazy circles overhead.

Eventually he heard a whistle from the trees. He got to his feet and stretched, his body bending like a bow. Then he sprinted down the hill . . . except, in the fading light, it didn't quite look like a sprint.

If he were a boy of ten, it would have looked like skipping. But he was no boy. If he were a goat, it would have looked like he were prancing. But he was no goat. If a man headed down the hill that quickly, it would have looked like he were running. Bast looked not quite like any of these, but in the fading light, there was in him some odd combination of the three.

In this way, Bast came to the edge of the clearing where Rike stood in the growing dark beneath the trees.

"I've got it," the boy said triumphantly, he held up his hand, but the needle was invisible in the fading light.

"Borrowed?" Bast asked. "Not traded or taken?"

Rike nodded earnestly.

"Okay," Bast said. "Let's see the stone as well."

Rike dug into his pocket and held it out.

Bast didn't take it, but made a show of looking it over, nodding seriously. He even went so far as to have the boy turn it over, so he could scrutinize the other side while he rubbed his chin. "Yes," Bast said at last, as if coming to a hard decision. "Yes. Very good. This will do."

Rike's breath gusted out in relief, and he tried to press the stone into Bast's hand.

Ever the artist, Bast recoiled as if the boy had tried to hand him a hot coal.

"I . . . thought you wanted it." Rike stuttered nervously, his face gone pale.

"It's not for *me*," Bast said. "The charm is only going to work for one person. That's why you needed to gather it yourself." Bast glanced up at the sky, and saw he had time enough to indulge himself a bit before he had to head back to the inn. He was proud of all he'd done today, but the difference between finish and flourish . . . well, that was something only artists know. Why craft and wrap a gift and then forsake the bow?

Bast leaned forward, lowering his voice. "The charm is so much more than just the parts," he said. "Most folk don't know it truly starts only when you understand your heart of hearts." Bast tapped the boy's chest lightly with two fingers.

"A true charm puts down roots in your desire," Bast continued, dancing back and forth between the truth and what folk thought was true. Making sure the boy would swallow it down smooth. "When you decided what you wanted, that's where it began. You've gone and gathered pieces proper as you can. Now we put a pin through it, so the whole thing sticks."

Bast made a gesture as if throwing something away. "Charms made any other way are naught but silly tricks." He nodded then, rather pleased with himself. This boy was nowhere near as sharp as Kostrel, but even so, he might stop to wonder why the "soon" he'd begged and bargained for seemed to begin before he'd actually made the charm itself.

The boy brought his hand back to his chest and eyed the stone. "What do you mean it only works for one person?"

That was what the boy was focused on? Bast fought the urge to sigh. So much of what he wrought was wasted here. "It's the way of charms," Bast lied. "They only work for one person at a time." Seeing the boy's confusion plain on his face, Bast sighed. "You know how folk make come-hither charms when they want to catch someone's eye?"

Rike nodded, blushing a little.

"This is the opposite," Bast said. "It's a go-thither charm. You're going to prick your finger, get a drop of your blood on it, and that will seal it. It will make things go away."

Rike looked down at the stone. "What sort of things?" he said.

"Anything that wants to hurt you," Bast extemporized. "You can just keep it in your pocket, or you can get a piece of cord—"

"But it will make my da leave?" Rike interrupted, his brow furrowing a bit in concern.

"Well, yes . . ." Bast said, his patience fraying at the interruptions. "That's what I said. You're his blood. So it will push him away more strongly than anything else. You'll probably want to hang it around your neck so—"

"What about a bear?" Rike asked, looking at the stone thoughtfully. "Would it make a bear leave me alone?"

Bast paused at that, realizing the last thing he needed was for this already rash and semi-feral child to think that he was safe from bears. "Wild things are different," he said. "They're possessed of pure desire. They don't want to *hurt* you. They usually want food, or safety. A bear would—"

"Can I give it to my mum?" Rike interrupted again, looking up at Bast. His dark eyes serious.

"—want to protect its terr . . . What?" Bast stumbled to a halt.

"My mum should have it," Rike said with sudden certainty. "What if I was off away with the charm and my da came back?"

"He's going farther away than that," Bast said, his voice heavy with certainty. "It's not like he'll be hiding around the corner at the smithy . . . ."

Rike's face was set now, his pug nose making him seem all the more stubborn. He shook his head. "My ma should have it. She's important. She has to take care of Tess and little Bip."

Bast waved a hand. "It will work just fi—"

"It's got to be for HER!" Rike shouted, suddenly furious, his hand making a fist around the stone. "You said it was for one person, so you make it be for her!"

Bast scowled at the boy. "I don't like your tone," he said grimly. "You asked me to make your da go away, and that's what I'm doing. . . ."

"But what if it's not enough?" Rike's voice was quieter, but his face was red.

"It will be," Bast said. He absentmindedly rubbed a thumb across the torn knuckles of his hand. "He'll go far away, and soon. You have my word—"

"NO!" Rike said, his face going red and angry. "What

if sending *him* en't enough? What if I grow up like my da? I get so . . ." His voice choked off, and his eyes started to leak tears. "I'm not good. I know it. I know better than anyone. Like you said. I got his blood in me. She needs to be safe. From me. If I grow up all twisted, she needs the charm to . . . she needs something to make me go a—"

Rike clenched his teeth, unable to continue.

Bast reached out and took hold of the boy's shoulder. He was stiff and rigid as a plank of wood. Slowly Bast gathered him in, and gently put his arms around his shoulders. They stood there for a long moment, Rike stiff as a bowstring, trembling like a sail tight against the wind.

"Rike," Bast said softly. "You're a good boy. Do you know that?"

The boy bent then, sagged against Bast and seemed like he would break himself apart with sobbing. His face was pressed into Bast's stomach and he said something, but it was muffled and disjointed. Bast made a soft crooning sound of the sort you'd use to calm a horse or soothe a hive of restless bees.

The storm passed and Rike stepped away, scrubbing

roughly at his face with his sleeve. The red sunset had spread, streaking the entire sky with shreds of pink and crimson.

"Right," Bast said, looking up at the sky. "It's time. We'll make it for your mother."

•••◦◗◉◖◦•••

They went down to the bank of the stream where they could both have a drink, and Rike could wash his face and collect himself a bit. When the boy's face was cleaner, Bast noted not all the smudginess was dirt. It was easy to make the mistake. The summer sun had tanned the boy a rich nut brown, and there had been no shortage of dirt. Even after he was clean, it was hard to tell they were the remains of bruises.

But despite the rumors, Bast's eyes were sharp. Even in the fading light he saw them, now that he was looking. Cheek and jaw. A darkness all around one skinny wrist. And when Rike bent to take a drink from the stream, Bast caught a glimpse of the boy's back. . . .

Bast was uncharacteristically silent as he led the boy back to the greystone at the base of the hill. Rike followed wordlessly when Bast climbed up one side of the half-fallen stone. Both of them had plenty of space to stand on the stone's broad back.

Rike looked around anxiously, as if worried someone might see them. But they were the only ones there. It was the hinge of the day, the time when all the town's children were running back to dinner, racing to make it home before night settled fully overhead.

They faced each other standing on the great grey stone, the tall dark shape that looked very like a man. The small dark shape that looked quite like a boy.

"There are some changes we'll have to make so it will fit your mother," Bast said without preamble. "You'll have to give it to her. River stone works best if it's given as a gift."

Rike nodded seriously, looking down at the stone in his hand. "What if she won't wear it?" he asked quietly.

Bast blinked, confused. "She'll wear it because you gave it to her," he said.

"What if she doesn't?" he asked.

Bast opened his mouth, then hesitated and closed it again. He looked up just in time to see the first of twilight's stars emerge. He looked down at the boy. He sighed. He wasn't good at this.

So much of this was easy. Hearts were easier to read than books. Glamour wasn't that much more than making sure folk saw the thing they already had plans to see. And making fools of foolish folk was hardly cunning grammarie.

But this? Convincing someone of the truth they were too twisted up to see? How could Bast begin to loosen such a knot?

It was baffling. These creatures, fraught and frayed in their desire. A snake would never poison itself, but these folk made an art of it. They wrapped themselves in fears and wept at being blind. It was infuriating. It was enough to break a heart.

So Bast took the easy way.

"It's part of the charm," he lied. "When you give it to her, you have to tell her that you made it for her because you love her."

The boy looked uncomfortable, as if he were trying to swallow a stone.

"It's the only way for it to work properly," Bast said firmly. "And if you want the magic to be strong, you need to tell her that you love her every day. Once in the morning and once at night."

The boy drew a deep breath, steeling himself before he nodded, a determined look on his face. "Okay. I can do that."

"Right then," Bast said. "First, say your father's name."

"Jessom Williams," Rike said, looking like he'd rather spit.

Bast nodded. "Sit down here. Prick your finger."

The two of them sat opposite each other, both cross-legged on the greystone. Bast put his handkerchief down, and Rike lay the dark river-stone on it before taking the needle and jabbing his finger.

Picking up the stone again, Rike watched intently as a bead of blood welled, then fell onto the surface of the smooth dark stone.

"Three drops," Bast said, matter-of-factly.

The boy let two more fall, then rubbed it in. In the fading light, the stone's dark color didn't change at all.

Bast picked up the handkerchief, but when he looked back up to hand it to the boy, he froze at what he saw.

Standing stark against the vibrant twilight sky, just over the boy's shoulder, stood the black-tipped finger of the lightning tree. Rising just above Rike's head, the crescent moon. It hung there like a sickle blade. A bowl.

It hung above the boy's head, bright as iron. It rested like a crown, like horns. Of course.

Bast laughed then, it burst from him, wild and delighted. He laughed again, it sounded like children playing in the water, like bells and birds, like someone breaking chains.

He grinned at Rike, and though he did not know it, in that moment Bast looked every bit the demon.

Bast held out his hand, his smile wide and white, the mad laughter bubbling up around the edges of his voice. "Good!" he said, a note of triumph ringing there. "Give me the needle!"

Rike hesitated. "You said it just needed—"

Bast laughed again. He knew he shouldn't, but there were times when it was either laugh or break wide open because he was too full. It would have been like holding back a sneeze. Sometimes the world was so perfectly revealed to be a joke, a picture, and a puzzle all at once. Laughter was the true applause you offered to the world for being beautiful.

And if there was some small applause still left for him, then that was only fair. It wasn't nothing, managing to find your way into alignment with the perfect seam of everything. But if you had the craft to see that's where you were? Well then you pick. You rip the seam or sew. That's when you learned the sort of artist that you truly were.

"Don't tell me what I said." But while Bast's voice was high and wild, it was not sharp or hard. He glanced up at the sky. It was purpling into twilight. "Hold the stone flat so that the hole faces up."

Rike did.

"And the needle."

Rike held it out. Bast took hold of it with terrible deliberate care, as if he gripped a nettle. As if his thumb and finger held a snake.

He closed his eyes and listened to Rike's breath, the breeze. His place. He heard the slow roll of the stream that circled deasil round the bottom of the hill. He felt it flowing in his bones, turning to the making way.

Grinning, Bast opened his eyes again. "Hold it steady."

In the fading light, Rike stared at him. Bast's eyes were dark as dark. He smiled like a child who knew that he was clever, quick, and wild enough to steal the moon.

Bast drove the needle hard into his thumb. A bead of blood swelled up. He turned his hand so it moved oddly

in the air. The black drop hung a moment before falling through the center of the charm to strike the greystone underneath.

There was no sound. No stirring in the air. No distant thunder. The most that could be said is that the night was somewhat still.

"Is that it?" Rike asked after a moment, clearly expecting something more.

"That's well begun," Bast said, licking the blood from his thumb. Then he worked his mouth a little and spat out the beeswax he'd been chewing. He rolled it round between his fingers and handed it to Rike. "Rub this into the stone, then you need to go sit by the lightning tree."

Rike peered up toward the final bit of sunset in the sky. "I . . . my ma will wonder where I am."

Bast nodded approvingly. "You're right to think on that. But we still have the rest to do." He pointed up toward the tree. "You know what a vigil is?"

Rike nodded numbly, seeming less certain than before.

"This is the second part. You need to sit a vigil with your charm," Bast said. "You hold your charm, and wait for me. Think on who you are, and who you want to be. And when you've thought on that, you think on how you love your ma." Bast looked up again. "The third part will come after, when the moon is higher in the sky."

Rike pushed himself to his feet, and started walking up the hill.

Bast leapt lightly from the greystone and was quickly lost among the trees.

TWILIGHT: CARROTS

BAST WAS HALFWAY back to the Waystone Inn when he realized he had no idea where his carrots were.

NIGHT: DEMONS

WHEN BAST CAME through the back door of the inn, he was greeted with the smell of baking bread, dark beer, and pepper in the simmering stew. Looking around the kitchen he saw crumbs on the breadboard and the lid off the kettle. Dinner had already been served.

Stepping softly, he peered through the door into the common room. The usual folk sat hunched at the bar. There was Old Cob and Graham, scraping their bowls. The smith's prentice was running bread along the inside of his bowl, stuffing it into his mouth a piece at a time.

Jake spread butter on the last slice of bread, and Shep knocked his empty mug politely against the bar, the hollow sound a question in itself.

Bast bustled through the doorway with a fresh bowl of stew for the smith's prentice as the innkeeper poured Shep more beer. Collecting the empty bowl, Bast disappeared back into the kitchen, then he came back with another loaf of bread half-sliced and steaming.

"Guess what I caught wind of today?" Old Cob said with the smug grin of a man who knew he had the best news at the table.

"What's that?" the smith's prentice asked around half a mouthful of stew.

Old Cob reached out and took the heel of the bread, a right he claimed as the oldest person there, despite the fact that he wasn't actually the oldest, and the fact that no one else much liked the heel. Bast suspected he took it because he was proud he still had so many teeth left.

Cob grinned. "Guess," he said to the boy, then slathered his bread with butter and took a bite.

"I reckon it's something about Jessom Williams," Jake said blithely.

Old Cob glared at him, his mouth full of bread and butter.

"What I heard," Jake drawled slowly, smiling as Old Cob tried furiously to chew his mouth clear. "Was that Jessom was out running his trap lines and he got jumped by a cougar. Then while he was legging it away, he lost track of hisself and ran straight over Littlecliff. Busted himself up something fierce."

Old Cob finally managed to swallow, "You're thick as a post, Jacob Walker. Who said it was a cougar?"

Jake paused a bit too long before saying, "It just makes sense—"

"I don't know what it is with you and cougars," Old Cob said, scowling at him. "Jessom was just drunk off his feet is what I heard. That's the only sense of it. Cause Littlecliff en't nowhere near his trap line. Unless you think a cougar chased him almost two whole miles . . ."

Old Cob sat back in his chair then, smug as a judge.

Jake glared venomously at Old Cob, but before he could make some further argument for cougars, Graham chimed in. "A couple kids found him while they were playing by the falls. They thought he was dead and ran to fetch the constable. But turns out he was just head-struck and drunk as a lord. The little girl said he smelled like drink, and he was cut up from some broken glass there, too."

Old Cob threw his hands up in the air. "Well ain't

that wonderful!" he said, scowling back and forth between Graham and Jake. "Any other parts of my story you'd like to tell afore I'm finished?"

Graham looked taken aback. "I thought you were—"

"I wasn't finished," Cob said, as if talking to a simpleton. "I was reelin it out slow. Tehlu anyway. What you folk don't know about tellin stories would fit into a book."

A tense silence settled among the friends.

"I got some news too," the smith's prentice said almost shyly. He sat slightly hunched at the bar, as if embarrassed at being a head taller than everyone else and twice as broad across the shoulders. "If'n nobody else has heard it, that is."

Shep spoke up. "Go on, Boy. You don't have to ask. Those two just been gnawing on each other for years. They don't mean anything by it."

The smith's prentice nodded, not blinking at being called 'boy' despite the fact that he did the lion's share of the town's smithing these days, and had been drinking with the other men for two years.

"Well I was doing shoes," the smith's prentice said. "When Crazy Martin came in." The boy shook his head in amazement and took a long drink of beer. "I ain't only seen him but a few times in town, and I forgot how big he is. I don't hardly have to look up to see him, but I still think he's biggern me. And today he was spittin nails. I swear. He looked like someone had tied two angry bulls together and made them wear a shirt!" The boy laughed the easy, too-large laughter of someone who's had a little more beer than they're used to.

There was a pause. "And what's the news then?" Shep asked gently, giving him a nudge.

"Oh!" the smith's prentice said. "He came asking Master Ferris if he had enough copper to mend a big kettle." The prentice spread his long arms out wide, one hand almost smacking Shep in the face.

"Apparently someone found his still." The smith's prentice leaned forward, wobbling slightly, and said in hushed voice, "Stole a bunch of his drink and wrecked up the place a bit." The boy leaned back in his chair and crossed his arms proudly across his chest, confident of a story well told.

But there was none of the buzz that normally accompanied a piece of good gossip. The boy took another drink of beer, and slowly began to look confused.

"Tehlu anyway," Graham said, his face gone pale. "Martin'll kill him."

"What?" the prentice said, looking around and blinking like an owl. "Who?"

"Jessom, you tit," Jake snapped. He tried to cuff the boy on the back of his head, but couldn't reach it and had to settle for his shoulder instead. "The fellow who got skunk drunk in the middle of the day and fell off a cliff?"

"I thought it was a cougar," Old Cob said spitefully.

"He'll wish it was ten cougars when Martin gets him," Jake said grimly.

"What?" The smith's prentice laughed. "Crazy Martin? He's addled, sure, but he ain't *mean*. Month ago he cornered me and talked bollocks about barley for two hours," he laughed again. "About how it was healthful. How wheat would ruin a man. How money was dirty. How it chained you to the earth or some nonsense."

The prentice dropped his voice and hunched his shoulders a bit, widening his eyes and doing a passable Crazy Martin impression. "*You know?*" he said, making his voice rough and darting his eyes around. "*Yeah. You know. You hear what I'm sayin?*"

The prentice laughed again, a little more loudly than

he would have if he were strictly sober. "People think they have to be afraid of big folk, but they don't. I never hit a man in my life."

Everyone just stared at him. Their eyes were deadly earnest.

"Martin killed one of Ensal's dogs on market day a couple years back," Shep said. "Right in the middle of street. Threw a shovel like it was a spear."

"Nearly killed that last priest," Graham said into his mug before taking a drink. "The one before Abbe Leodin. Nobody knows why. Fellow went up to Martin's house. That evening Martin brought him to town in a wheelbarrow and left him in front of the church. Broke his jaw. Some ribs and such. He didn't wake up for three days." He looked at the smith's prentice. "That was before your time though. Makes sense you wouldn't know."

"Punched a tinker once," Jake said.

"*Punched a tinker?*" the innkeeper burst out, incredulous.

"Reshi," Bast said gently. "Martin is fucking *crazy*."

Jake nodded. "Even the levy man doesn't go up to Martin's place."

Cob looked like he was going to call Jake out again,

then decided to take a gentler tone. "Well yes," he said. "True enough. But that's cause Martin pulled his full rail in the king's army. Eight years."

"And came back mad as a frothing dog," Shep said, but he said it quietly.

Old Cob was already off his stool and halfway to the door. "Enough talk. We got to let Jessom know. If he can get out of town until Martin cools down a bit . . ."

"So . . . when he's dead?" Jake said. "Remember when he threw a horse through the window of the old inn because the barman wouldn't give him another beer?"

"A *tinker*?" the innkeeper repeated, sounding no less shocked than before.

Silence descended at the sound of footsteps on the landing. Eyeing the door, everyone went still as stone, except for Bast who edged toward the doorway to the kitchen.

Everyone breathed a huge sigh of relief when the door opened to reveal the tall, slim shape of Carter. He closed the door behind him, not noticing the tension in the room. "Guess who's standing a round of bottle whiskey for everyone tonight?" he called out cheerfully, then stopped where he stood, confused by the room full of grim expressions.

Old Cob started to walk to the door again, motioning

for his friend to follow. "Come on Carter, we'll explain on the way. We've got to go find Jessom double-quick."

"You'll have a long ride to find him," Carter said. "Seeing as I drove him all the way to Baedn tonight."

Everyone in the room seemed to relax. "That's why you're so late," Graham said, his voice thick with relief. He slumped back onto his stool and tapped the bar with a knuckle. Bast drew him another beer.

Carter frowned. "Not so late as all that," he groused. "All the way to Baedn and back. Even with a dry road and an empty cart I made damn good time . . ."

Old Cob put a hand on the man's shoulder. "Nah. It ain't like that," he said, steering his friend toward the bar. "We were just a little spooked. You probably saved that damn fool's life getten him out of town." He squinted. "Though I've told you, you shouldn't be out on the road by yourself these days."

The innkeeper fetched Carter a bowl while Bast went outside to tend to his horse. While he caught up on dinner, his friends told him the day's gossip in dribs and drabs.

"Well that explains it," Carter said. "Jessom showed up reeking like a rummy and looking like he'd been beat by seven different demons."

"Only seven?" Bast asked.

Carter took a drink and seemed to give the question more thought than it deserved. "Yeah. But all different demons, mind you. Like one that had a real love for knuckles, and another who came at him with a switch, and . . ." He trailed off, frowning as he realized he couldn't seem to think of more than two types of demon.

"And one who would go after him with a bottle," Shep said helpfully. He'd traveled a bit in his youth as a caravan guard, and had seen some fairly rough business.

"And one who puts the boot in once they get him down!" the smith's prentice chimed in cheerfully, raising his mostly empty mug.

"Can't imagine there's a demon who would only want a switch," Graham mused to Jake. "Seems like short beer there."

"I'd take a fair shot in the gut before a proper switching," Jake replied philosophically. "My old gran couldn't hardly lift a cat, but she'd clip me so's I'd see stars."

". . . right in the nadgers!" the smith's prentice added, making an enthusiastic motion with one foot.

Old Cob cleared his throat and the conversation stilled. "Let's assume it was an appropriately varied group of demons," he said, eyeing the lot of them sternly before gesturing for Carter to continue.

"Numbers aside," Carter conceded, "what demons there were sure put in their penny's worth. He was a proper mess, something wrong with his arm, limping. Asked me to drive him to the Iron Hall, and he took the king's coin right there."

Carter took a drink of beer. "Then he changed his coin and offered me double to drive him straightaway to Baedn. Asked him if he wanted to stop for clothes or anything, but he seemed in a good hurry."

"No need to pack a bag," Shep said. "They'll dress and feed him in the king's army."

Graham let out a sigh. "That was a near miss. Can you imagine what would happen if Martin got hold of him?"

"Imagine what would happen if the azzie came for Martin," Jake said darkly.

Everyone was silent for a moment. Folk died sometimes. But outright murder meant the Crown's law. It was all too easy to imagine the trouble that would come if an officer of the Crown was assaulted here in town while attempting to arrest Crazy Martin.

The smith's prentice looked around at everyone's

expressions. "What about Jessom's family?" he asked, plainly worried. "Will Martin come after them?"

The men at the bar shook their heads in concert. "Martin is crazy," Old Cob said. "But he's not that sort. Not to go after a woman or her wee ones."

"I heard he punched that tinker because he was making himself familiar with young Jenna," Graham said.

The group grumbled indistinctly at that, sounding like thunder in the distance.

After it faded, there was a moment's quiet. "Nah," Old Cob said softly. "Weren't that."

Everyone in the room turned to look at him, surprised. They'd known Cob all their lives, enough to hear every story he knew. The idea that he might have held something back was almost unthinkable.

"I caught the tinker after he'd done most of his trading," Cob said, not looking up from his beer. "I'd waited, as I wanted to ask after some items . . . they were personal-like." He paused for a moment, then sighed and shrugged. "He ran his mouth a bit on the subject." Cob swallowed. "And . . . well, you know me. I told him he better mind his tone."

The old man went quiet again. "And he sort of . . . pushed me. And I weren't expecting it, so I fell over. And he . . . well . . . he hit me a bit." The smoke in the fireplace made more noise than the other men in the room, as Old Cob rolled his mug idly in his hands, still not looking up. "Said a few things too. Can't say's I remember the details too clear though."

A shadow of a smile curled up on the old man's face, as he glanced up from his beer. "Then Martin came round the corner." He shared a look with Jake and Graham. "Y'all know how Martin gets himself all in a puzzle sometimes?"

Jake bobbed his head. "Caught me in my garden once. Asked why my fenceposts weren't square. I couldn't half guess what he meant, and not a thing I said made sense to him. But he kept on like a dog chewing its own leg. Talked the sun down. Couldn't understand. Couldn't seem to walk away, either."

Cob touched his nose. "That's the thing," he said. "Never seen a man who could get his wheels in a rut like Martin. But this particular night, Martin sees me there with this big bastard standing up over me, blood on his knuckles . . ." Cob shook his head at the memory. "He wasn't in a puzzle then. No talking. Not a blink. Martin doesn't even break stride. He just turns a bit and walks up to the tinker."

Old Cob chuckled a bit with grim satisfaction. "It was like a hammer hitting a ham. Knocked the fellow right out into the street. Ten feet, my hand to god. Then Martin looked at me laying there like a beetle on my back, and he walks over to the fellow and sticks the boot in good and hard." He gave a nod of acknowledgment to the smith's prentice. "Good and solid, but nowhere near as hard as he *could* have. And just once. Look on his face was the damnedest thing. I could tell he was just settling up accounts in his head. Like a moneylender shimming up his scale."

"That wasn't any kind of proper tinker," Jake said with a low note in his voice. "I remember him."

A few of the others nodded wordlessly. They each took a careful moment to let time pass and drink their drinks.

"What if Jessom comes back?" the smith's prentice asked. "I heard some folk get drunk and take the coin, then turn all cowardly and jump the rail when they sober up."

Everyone paused to consider that. A band of the king's guard had come through town only last month and posted a notice, announcing a reward for deserters from the army.

"Tehlu anyway," Shep said grimly. "Wouldn't that be a great royal pisser of a mess?"

"Jessom's not coming back," Bast said dismissively. His voice had such a note of absolute certainty that everyone turned to eye him.

Bast tore off a piece of bread and put it in his mouth before he realized he was the center of attention. He swallowed awkwardly and made a broad gesture with both hands. "What?" he asked them, laughing. "Would *you* come back, knowing Martin was waiting?"

There was a chorus of negative grunts and shaken heads.

"You have to be a special kind of stupid to wreck up Martin's still," Old Cob said.

"Maybe eight years will be enough for Martin to cool down a bit," Shep said.

"Maybe I'll lend a prince a penny and he'll give it back," Jake said darkly. "But I'm not going to hold my breath."

MIDNIGHT: LESSONS

RIKE WAS SITTING solemnly at the base of the lightning tree when Bast returned. He climbed to his feet stiffly, looking up at Bast. "What now?" he asked.

Bast nodded. "That's a good question," he said somberly. "That is, in many ways, the only important question that there is."

Rike waited patiently, not saying anything.

"You remember our deal?" Bast asked the boy.

Rike was shaking just a little, though Bast couldn't guess if it was fear or weariness or chill. He nodded slowly. "Yes sir."

Bast blinked at that, just once. Then he looked up to see the moon directly overhead. Over the tree. Over the boy. "Now we do the most important part. You've had some time to think on it." Bast looked down at the boy. "So. Tell me who you think you are."

He had expected the boy to either blurt out some mess or shut up tighter than a clam, forcing Bast to drag an answer out of him.

But Rike surprised him. "I'm a liar," he said, his voice steady and grave. "I hate folk way too easy. I get angry all the time." Rike swallowed. "I wish a had a demon in my shadow, but I don't. I wish I were just worthless, but I'm worse. It en't like I'm good and there's sommat makes me bad," he looked down. "It's just me. I'm like my dad."

Bast inclined his head, acknowledging the answer without making any sign of agreement. "Tell me who you want to be."

Again there wasn't any hesitation. "I want to be the boy I was when it was just me and my ma," he said, sudden tears welling up and rolling down his face. "I don't want to feel like I feel anymore. I want to be the boy I was before."

Bast stepped closer then, the graceful motion subtly strange. Without meaning to, Rike tried to step away, but his back was already pressed tight against the smooth side of the bone-white tree.

Moving slowly, Bast bent down and put his face up close to Rike's. His eyes were black, the color of the moon when it was gone.

"I own you," Bast said. "Every part. Tongue and teeth. Name to nape of neck." It wasn't a question exactly, but something in his voice made it clear he expected a response.

The boy nodded woodenly.

Bast reached up to put one hand against the smooth side of the tree above Rike's head. He then walked slowly widdershins until he stood before the boy again. "The part of your father that lives in your shadow. That is mine. The fear that you will grow up into him. That's mine as well. The part of you that hates yourself, and feels that he was right to hate you. Those are mine. I'm taking them forever." His voice was like a chisel against stone. "Now."

Bast walked another ring around the boy. He moved against the world, the breaking way. "You aren't a liar," Bast said, "Say it."

Rike opened his mouth, then stopped.

Finishing this turn round the tree, Bast brought his face down close again. "You are just a boy who lied." His voice was like a whip. "Say it."

"I just lied," Rike said softly. "I en't a liar."

"You've done bad things," Bast said. "But you aren't bad." A pause. "Say it."

"I en't bad."

Slowly, as if pressing into wind or through deep water, Bast took the step that brought his third and final turning to a close. There was no wind. No cricket stitched. The night stood breathless as a balanced coin.

Bast stopped to stand before the boy. "You are not worse than worthless." He lowered his hand from the tree and lay it flat against Rike's chest, above his heart. Rike's eyes were shut, but even so, he could feel Bast leaning close.

"You are as precious as the moon." Bast's voice was soft and sure. Rike felt Bast's breath brush gently up against his face. It smelled like violets and honey.

Rike's mouth moved quietly, his eyes still closed.

Bast put his hand against the trunk and turned, moving round the tree the other way. His steps described a circle tight around the tree, around the boy, around the moon above. He moved in the direction of the turning world, the shaping way, the way that bent things to be more of what they were. And in this moment, in this place, Bast held his heart's desire like a nail that he would hammer hard into the world.

Another turning deasil. Stopping briefly, Bast rested the hand not against the tree atop Rike's head. "Think of everything you've done to keep them safe," he said. "You are brave, and strong, and full of love."

Fingers trailing lightly round the tree, Bast made his third turn of the making way. He finished his full circle, pulled his hand away, and knelt to fold the boy into his arms.

And last he gently whispered in Rike's ear, something so true only the boy could hear.

••••••••••

Bast waited for Rike at the bottom of the hill. He sat on the great fallen stone, and kicked his feet idly as he watched the glowflies try to flirt with stars reflected in the stream. Bast smiled and couldn't help but be impressed at the amazing aspiration. If only everyone could be so brave . . .

Watching Rike come slowly down the hill, Bast smiled in almost exactly the same way. Kostrel had been right. It was the easy way. You simply layered it, like cream on top of frosting on a cake.

Wordlessly, Bast hopped off the greystone and the two of them made their slow way through the moonlit wood, following the faintest trails that only deer and children know. Halfway there, Bast was surprised when Rike hesitantly reached up and took hold of his hand. Surprised but not displeased. He gave it a small squeeze without looking at the boy.

They cut through the Alsoms' orchard, but the apples were still small and green. They hopped a gully with an invisible trickling creek lost far below. They startled a possum, looked at the stars, and snuck beneath the ancient hedge that ran around the old abandoned mill.

They stayed together until they saw the amber lamplight in the window of his mother's house. Then Bast stopped and let Rike take the final steps himself.

••••◖●◗••••

It was late at the Waystone Inn, and the last of the customers were gone. It had been a later, livelier night than

normal, with all the news and Carter flush with extra coin.

But now, Bast and the innkeeper sat in the kitchen, making their own late dinner from the remainder of the stew and half a loaf of bread.

"So what did you learn today, Bast?" the innkeeper asked.

Bast grinned widely. "Today Reshi, I found out where Emberlee takes her bath!"

The innkeeper cocked his head thoughtfully. "Emberlee? The Alards' daughter?"

"Emberlee Ashton!" Bast threw his arms up into the air and made an exasperated noise. "She's only the third prettiest girl in twenty miles, Reshi!"

"Ah," the innkeeper said, an honest smile flickering across his face for the first time that day. "You'll have to point her out to me sometime."

Bast grinned. "I'll take you there tomorrow," he said excitedly. "She's sweet as cream and broad of beam." His smile grew to wicked proportions. "She's a milkmaid, Reshi." He said the last with heavy emphasis. "A *milkmaid*."

The innkeeper shook his head, even as a smile spread helplessly across his face. Finally he broke into a chuckle and held up his hand. "You can point her out to me some-time when she has her clothes on, Bast," he said stolidly. "That will do nicely."

Bast gave a disapproving sigh. "It would do you good to get out a bit, Reshi."

The innkeeper shrugged. "It's possible," he said as he poked idly at his stew.

They ate in silence for a long while. Bast tried to think of something to say.

"I did get the carrots, Reshi," Bast offered up as he ladled the last of the stew from the copper kettle into his bowl.

"Better late than never, I suppose," the innkeeper said. The brief laughter from before had already spilled out of him, leaving him listless and grey. "We'll use them to-morrow."

Bast shifted in his seat, embarrassed. "I might have lost them afterwards," he said sheepishly.

This wrung another smile from the innkeeper, tired but genuine. "Don't worry yourself over it, Bast." Then he paused, eyes narrowing as he focused on Bast's hand. "How did you hurt yourself?"

Bast looked down at the knuckles of his right hand.

They weren't bleeding any more, but the injury was still obvious. His left hand had come off better and was only slightly bruised.

"I fell out of a tree," Bast said. Not lying, but not answering the question, either. It was better not to lie outright. Even like this, a shadow of himself, his master was not an easy man to fool.

"You should be more careful, Bast," the innkeeper said, prodding listlessly at his food.

"I *was* careful, Reshi," Bast said. "I made sure to fall on the grass and everything."

This drew another smile from the innkeeper, but not much more than that. "As little as there is to do around here, Bast, it would be nice if you spent more time on your studies."

"I learned things today, Reshi," Bast protested.

The innkeeper glanced up. "Really?" he asked, failing to keep the skepticism out of his voice.

"Yes!" Bast said, his voice high and impatient. "Loads of things! *Important* things!"

The innkeeper raised an eyebrow then, his expression growing sharper. "Impress me then."

Bast thought for a moment, then leaned forward in

his chair. "Well," Bast said with conspiratorial intensity. "First and most important. I have it on very good authority that Nettie Williams discovered a wild hive of bees today." He grinned enthusiastically. "What's more, I hear she caught the queen. . . ."

AUTHOR'S ENDNOTE

Part One: Lumpy Nothing-Flavored Water

I'm going to be honest with y'all here.

Over the years, I've had a lot of trouble getting things written. On rare occasion, it's a fun sort of trouble. More of a challenge. Like trying to get your head around a riddle, or puzzling your way through an escape room.

But usually, it isn't entertaining in the slightest. It's like driving on a road full of deep potholes. Or trying to buy groceries during a tornado. Or like one of those dreams where you're trying to go somewhere important, but no matter how hard you run, you just can't seem to move . . . .

Revising this story for publication has been the first

sort of trouble. It ended up being *much* more complex than I'd anticipated. And while I felt guilty about how long it was taking, at every step I could *feel* the story getting better. Much better. So the extra trouble felt worthwhile . . .

But this author's note? It's been the second type of trouble. I put it off until the end of all the edits and my art direction because I thought it would be easy. Instead, here I am, trying to write it one more time almost a month after I meant to have it done.

The problem isn't the writing itself. I've written, at my best guess, between 8,000 and 10,000 words of things I hoped would be an author's note. I told the story of how "The Lightning Tree" came to be, then came to be something new. I wrote about my misadventures trying to come up with a new title. Musings about the nature of faerie tales. Something that turned into an essay about cultural universality of fortune-telling and an explanation of how Embrils came to exist in Temerant. Interesting asides. Philosophical snippets. Amusing anecdotes.

But no matter how I brought those things together, it didn't work.

Odds are, you aren't an author, so I'll try and put this in another context.

Imagine going to the store, buying chicken and potatoes and carrots, then picking a bunch of fresh herbs, then spending all day making soup. You add salt and pepper and garlic. All things you enjoy. All things you know taste good. All things that *should* combine to make delicious soup.

And at the end, after all that work, despite everything, what you end up with is warm, lumpy, nothing-flavored water.

That's been my last month. I keep bringing together bits that should make an author's note, and instead I get long swath of lumpy, nothing-flavored text. It's equal parts infuriating, frustrating, and terrifying.

So here I am. I have to finish this today. I've promised myself, my publisher, and my children.

My plan is what you're seeing here. First, I'm going to be honest with you. I wanted to give you a really excellent author's note. I wanted it to be entertaining, informative, thoughtful, clever, charming, insightful, funny, engaging, and delightful. I wanted it to hang a smile on your heart and make you forget the woes of the world. That's the author's note you deserve.

But I can't seem to do that. I'm sorry. Imma do my best here, and I'm sorry if it's not as good as any of us hoped.

The second piece of my plan is (I hope) ingenious: I'm going to fall back on the one thing I can always do no matter how hard my day has been. The one thing that I've never gotten tired of over the years. The one thing that always delights me.

I'm going to tell some stories about my kids.

Part Two: What My Children Have Taught Me About Stories

Let's set the stage. Here are the Dramatis Personae:

Oot: My older boy. Early teen-ish. Precocious. Empathetic. Considerate. Long blond hair. My sweet little Viking boy.

Cutie: My younger boy. Ten-ish. Precocious. Empathetic. Impish. Long blond hair. My sweet little angel baby.

●●●▶◗◉◖◀●●●

Back when Oot was around two years old, I told him many stories. But one of his favorites was the story of The Big Bad Wolf.

It's the gold-standard for kid stories. It has *everything*. It's the entire package.

I can actually sense-memory back to telling Oot this story. Him sitting in our big bed, just a little pink potato in a diaper, looking up at me. He'd listen and ask for it again and again. Because if you didn't know, kids *love* hearing the same story over and over. And over.

Then one day, after I'd done an especially good job huffing and puffing (if I do say so myself), he looked at me and said in the broken-English baby talk that I understood perfectly. "Tell about the big GOOD wolf?"

It hit me like a thunderbolt. He loved this story, and, as we've already established, kids love hearing the same thing again and again. And again. If you've ever read to a kid, you know how bad this can get. They'll call you out if you miss a single word in a story they love.

Nevertheless, I knew exactly what he was saying. I knew what he MEANT. I suddenly imagined him like a little movie producer giving me notes on my first draft of a screenplay. "Pat. Baby. Bubeleh. I love what you've sent me. It's perfect. Drama! Brotherhood! The huffing. The puffing. Love it! Straw then sticks, *then* bricks? What a twist! And the moral at the end! Chef's kiss! You're a miracle worker!"

He pauses then, in my little imagining. He picks his next words carefully, not wanting to offend me . . . .

"But this wolf. He eats these pigs. Right? And they're, like, talking sentient creatures. Don't you think that's a little fucked up? I mean, I'm a kid and you're telling me a story with the equivalent of a serial killer. I love how clever the final pig is at the end. He's obviously the clever one. You established that with the bricks. But tricking the wolf down the chimney into a pot of boiling water. Are you trying to normalize torture and retributive murder? Where's my happily ever after? Are you trying to sell vigilante justice to a two year old? I mean, he's supposed to be pig-man. Not Batman. Am I right?"

And he was right. He was telling me he loved the story, but why did the wolf have to be a dick? More to the point, why did the wolf have to be a cannibal murderer whose behavior was so egregious that it could only be stopped by one of the most horrific deathtraps possible?

What he was asking for was, effectively, a story without all the conflict. Without tension and animosity. Without many of the things I'd been taught were *essential* to story-telling.

This wasn't a totally new idea to me. I'd already spent 14 years writing a fantasy novel without a single sword-fight, goblin army, or looming apocalypse. I had specifically avoided having a god-lion tortured to death, or farm boys straight-up murk any tyrants or mad wizards. Nobody destroyed anything in a volcano thereby ruining magic forever and making all the elves sad enough to fuck off forever out of the world.

I'd always suspected that a good story didn't *need* stakes that high. I wrote *The Name of the Wind* with that as one of my driving philosophies, and given how many people read it and recommended it to their friends, there's some decent data showing I was right.

But it was there, laying in bed, that my little boy of two proved conclusively that we *aren't* born bloodthirsty little monsters, addicted to acrimony and strife.

It was then and there that I learned down in my bones that stories could be kind and gentle while still being enjoyable. More of them should be. We love the huffing and puffing. We love the bricks. Why not leave behind the belief that there needs to be a bad wolf, or even a bad anything? Why not give us a good wolf instead?

And it's literally only now, typing this, that I realize that's what Bast is. He's a good wolf.

(I don't know about you. But I feel like this author's note is going pretty well so far. I'm excited.)

●●●●●●●●

Fast forward almost a decade. I've gotten into the habit of reading to my boys at night. All the Little House on the Prairie books. Some of Narnia. Willy Wonka (twice). *The Hobbit* (three times). *The Last Unicorn. The Graveyard Book.* And others, a wild eclectic smattering of various genres and time periods.

We'd started reading one of the old classics I'd been excited to bring to the boys. And while they liked it well enough, they weren't enthralled. And, to my dismay, I wasn't either. I was also surprised how hard it was to read aloud. The book was over sixty years old, and a lot of the sentence structure . . . Let's just say it really didn't roll off the tongue.

So we decided to switch books, and since I was thinking in terms of reading out loud, I jokingly mentioned I could read them one of *my* books. Specifically, *The Slow Regard of Silent Things*.

They were *very* excited at the thought. Startlingly excited. And I immediately regretted bringing it up. I felt awkward for some reason, though I was hard pressed to explain why.

More importantly, *Slow Regard* is a strange book. Don't

get me wrong. I love it. But it's a book where nothing happens. It's less a story and more a 30,000 word vignette. No traditional action. Or plot. Or dialogue. I once heard it described as "the story of a sad girl who picks things up and puts them down again," and while that's not particularly flattering, it's 100% true.

But my boys were oddly enthusiastic. So I caved and offered a compromise. I'd read for 10 minutes. If they didn't like it, or if I felt too weird, we could stop and there wouldn't be any hard feelings either way.

So we lay down in bed and I started to read. Much to my surprise, it didn't feel odd. I had done the audiobook back in the day, and I was right in remembering that it was easy, even fun, to read out loud.

What's more, the boys were *very* into it. Like, on-the-edge-of-their-seats. They were intent and engaged with this odd, small story of a girl all on her own, thinking her thoughts and trying to move gently through her little underground world.

So I kept reading, and we got to the scene where Auri is swimming and Foxen slips from her fingers.

And Cutie, who is snuggled under the covers, supposed to be getting warm and drowsy and ready for sleep, instead sits bolt upright in bed. "Oh no!" he exclaims. His body is vibrating, his voice high, full of genuine distress. "They've been together FOREVER!"

We'd only been reading for 20 minutes. He didn't know a single thing about my world or these characters.

Over the years, I've received a lot of good reviews. I've won awards. Hit bestseller lists. My books have sold over ten million copies in over 35 languages. I've had book signings with thousands of people. One in Madrid lasted for 14 hours. I've been guest of honor at a dozen conventions. Once, I was hugged by both Felicia Day and Neil Gaiman *in the same day.*

What I'm getting at here is that I have lived a rich, full life. I have my fair share of lauds and plaudits. And while I consider myself mostly a failure professionally, as I'm unproductively obsessive, inconsistent, and unpunctual, I've known for a long while that I'm good at doing words. I'm proud of my writing.

Nevertheless, when my younger boy sat up in bed, so obviously distressed, so obviously emotionally invested in Auri and Foxen despite having only known them for 16 pages. . . . I remember thinking, "I'm good at this," in a new, different way.

It made me view *Slow Regard* in a different light, too. Not as an odd side project a few people might like because they were already fans of my work. But as something anyone could enjoy. As a gentle story that somehow still felt important and emotionally true. It was something I was proud of bringing into the world.

If not for that, I don't think I would have felt justified in coming back to improve and revise "The Lightning Tree." I certainly wouldn't have done the revision equivalent of starting to replace the wallpaper in the hallway, only to have the project snowball until I've pulled down all the drywall, replaced all the wiring and plumbing, and decided to tear out a wall to make space for a kitchen island.

Now that I've finished it, I'm so glad I did. Rike and Bast deserved better, and now they have it.

Part Three: An Open Letter to My Children

Hello there, my sweet boys.

Just now, I finished reading the above author's note to you to make sure you were comfortable with everything I've put in there. That you're okay with me sharing those things with the world. As we've talked about many times, consent is important.

I wrote this story long ago. Oot, you were very young, and Cutie, you were mostly conceptual. That means all the children in here were created long before I had much experience with kids. More importantly, I hadn't yet met the older versions of you.

This means a couple things.

First, none of them are based on you or things you've done or said. I mention this because I know folks will be tempted to draw parallels, or puzzle out what came from where. It's human nature. We want to unravel things and understand their origins. You might be tempted to do that yourself in the future, wondering if there was some commentary about you or your behavior buried in here. There isn't. Don't make yourself crazy looking for that.

Second, I just want to say I'm pretty proud of how good a job I did on these kids, given my lack of experience. They turned out pretty great, in my opinion. Apparently I'm good at making stuff up. Who knew?

Sixth and lastly, thank you for helping me write this book, even though you didn't know that's what you were doing. Thank you for letting me read the entire thing out loud to you while I was revising. It was such a joy to share it with you. Your reactions helped me fine-tune things, and reassured me that while the story has much that is hidden, none of the essentials were buried too deep.

Thirdly, thank you for being patient today. These summer days together are indescribably precious. The weather was lovely, our garden was ripe, we had plans to play a board game. I'd hoped to finish this author's note in about two hours . . . instead it has taken more than seven. You never complained or were anything other than perfectly gracious and understanding. You amaze me with your kindness and consideration. Even now I hear you downstairs, setting the table for dinner, talking and singing.

In conclusion, I want you to know this. As proud as I am of these kids that I created for this story, they don't hold a candle to you. You are so much more wild and wicked and wise. So much more clever and kind. You are amazing to such a degree, that if I told the world all there was to tell, they would not believe it was true. This is because you are fantastic in every sense of the world.

Those of you reading this who aren't my children? I appreciate you too. Thank you for your kindness and consideration. Thank you for your patience. Thank you.

Everyone out there reading this, especially my children, I hope you know this truth down in the middle of your bones: You are amazing. You are fantastic.

You are beautiful and brave and full of love.
You are as lovely as the moon.

—Pat Rothfuss
July, 2023

P.S. If you're curious about the author's notes I didn't use, I'll be posting some of them over on my blog at blog.patrickrothfuss.com.

A lot of what I wrote will surely go to the cider-apple heap, but I'd hate to lose the good bits. Like the story of how "The Lightning Tree" came into existence and eventually became this book. Some of the anecdotes about titles, revisions, or faerie tales hold up too. There's also an odd maunder about Robert Frost, spoilers, and the purpose of art that might bear saving. . . .

Best of all, there's a conversation where Nate Taylor and I tell stories and talk about how we do art together (spoiler: Nate does the art and I'm a nuisance). We also show off some early sketches so you can see how much things change, and take the opportunity to reveal some of the illustrations we loved, but still had to cut from the final version of the book.

ABOUT THE ILLUSTRATOR

Nate Taylor spent his childhood in snow caves and learned how to speak by watching *Star Trek*. He now lives with his family in the Pacific Northwest, where he freelances as a human illustrator, cartoonist, and portraitist.

ABOUT THE AUTHOR

Pat Rothfuss grew up wild in the forests of the midwest, raiding local libraries for sustenance and frightening tourists. He now lives mostly in Temerant, where he has a hard time taking things seriously, including writing his bio.